The Last Workshop

The Last Workshop

John Minichillo

ISBN: 978-1-948743-03-7

The Last Workshop

Publication: 2.0-print (First Edition), 2017.

HYBRID Ink, LLC
Independent Publishers of Thoughtful Writing

hybrid.ink
Everett, WA

Printed in the United States of America
10 9 8 7 6 5 4 3 2 1

I

Lydia's boss, the famous writer, tasked her with making contact with as many former students as she could find. This meant poring through file boxes of old graduate school applications to try to determine which students had been accepted, and whether they attended the program. Because when she asked her boss if she should limit her search to those who graduated, which would be easier, he said, simply, "No." As a writing program it wasn't the degree that mattered as much as the experience. A student who had dropped out may have continued to write and managed to make good. He wanted to hear of their successes, but he also just wanted to know where they all were. He wanted to make contact with them again, however slight.

Lydia created a list of names and she Googled everyone to determine if they had ever been a writer. For some she had come across stories they had published in online journals, but often the bio line would proclaim, "So and so lives in Petal Mississippi and is a student of the Deep South Writers Workshop." So these kids had made a splash while they were here, under her boss's tutelage, but they'd often gone off silently into the world with no way for Google to find them again. After so many dead ends she went back over the applications and discovered she could make phone calls to the person listed as an emergency contact, usually a parent or close family member. The phone calls went like this: "Yes, hello. My name is Lydia Barrow and I'm calling from the Deep South Writers Workshop. I'm trying to reach so-and-so who was a student of ours. They did such fine work while they were with us and we're putting together an anthology of the writing of former students. We just wanted to make sure so-and-so knew about it. Is there a contact address where we could send a letter, or a phone number or an e-mail address?" Sometimes this meant explaining what an anthology was, and this was a chance for Lydia to exaggerate the impact such a publication would have on so-and-so's future career as a writer. But most often the family members on the other end of the line were forthcoming and more than happy to tattle on the whereabouts of those who had once dreamed of being writers. They were working in restaurants, they were store managers, they wrote for nonprofit agencies and big-name corporations. They taught in high schools and universities. They switched careers and went back through more prestigious graduate schools to earn degrees in disciplines with better career prospects. So there were lawyers, social workers, software techs, and even a doctor—a real *medical* doctor, not the kind who doctored over language and letters. One kid had even gone back to run for mayor in his town. He'd lost, but he'd run a solid campaign, and the father at the end of the line, who sounded tired, his voice dry and his words muddied with the enduring fatigue that comes with old age—he pepped up when he talked about his son's unsuccessful bid for city patrician. His mind sharpened, his cadence sped a beat, and he spoke with beaming pride: "He had finally decided to *do* something with his life."

This was an attitude she'd often encountered from the parents of the starry-eyed. The value of a writing degree was doubtable or even contemptible. Lydia knew that if these parents saw what the school was actually like they'd feel even more justified and explicit in their critiques: with the worn-out buildings where all the liberal arts classes were taught, and likewise their offices, and even the office of *The Deep South Triannual*, one of the most respected literary magazines on the market, or so her boss had said.

Lydia's boss was a man who loved to make things difficult for those around him. He called this "joking around," but his jokes were often at the expense of someone else's feelings, and she'd seen him tightrope the line of verbal and psychological abuse with some of the students. Lydia could take anything he said because she saw right through him and could even bite back. He seemed to enjoy this, having a subordinate with some spunk, and she took this approach with him because it was in her nature but also because he'd hinted that his previous secretaries were unable to get along with him, and so he'd sent them packing.

It was with his abusive nature in mind that she started to wonder why he suddenly cared about all the young writers he'd come into contact with. At first, she supposed it was his getting old coupled with feelings of loneliness even as the literary establishment trumpeted his latest book. Though it wasn't until she'd gotten through to a former student on the phone that it all coalesced for her.

"Why is he asking about me now?" the former-student had said. "Is he dying?"

And without any evidence other than a vague suspicion that when he took afternoons off he was going to see an oncologist, she said, "Yes. He is."

"That's rich," the former-student said. "So the old atheist wants to apologize? And he's getting *you* to do it for him?"

"He hasn't told me to apologize," Lydia said. "He hasn't told me he's dying."

"But he is?"

"Yes."

"He didn't look well in his last author photo."

"He's not well."

"Shit. I did learn a lot from him. He was my only writing mentor, for whatever that's worth."

"He would like to hear it."

"I'm supposed to send a card or something?"

"I don't know what you're supposed to do. Maybe an email?"

"I can do that. Does he still work there? Have they tried to kick him out?"

"They've tried. Unsuccessfully. He still resides, prestigiously."

"Well, I'm sorry to hear it. About his dying. Are you holding up?"

"I'm fine. I'll be fine."

And then Lydia hung up the phone and she had a whole new tactic to get through to them. Her story was that the famous writer was dying. She made sure to tell them it was a secret and they couldn't say anything. He hadn't quite come to terms with his mortality and they absolutely did not want the story in the press. And so even if they brought up his cancer he might not acknowledge it, or he would deny it, but a few kind words would mean a lot to him.

And so Lydia's lie about the famous writer's terminal illness spread around the country through the networks of the people who knew him, and out of loyalty to him they only talked about his condition with their spouses or the old friends they knew during that time of their lives when they dropped everything to go live in Mississippi to learn to write fiction from a Minimal Realist, and they'd holed up in air-conditioned shotgun shacks where they wrote as if their lives depended on it.

§

When Allison Avett saw the email from Trent she dreaded opening it. His subject line was simply, "Important," and she had run out of delicate ways to tell him she didn't have the time to give him feedback on his latest novel manuscript. She admired his pluck. Despite sticking with the unpublishable name Trent Sanivaugh, he wrote more than anyone she knew, and she had a lot of writer friends. She had met all these other writers at conferences, retreats, and an exclusive Facebook group called Fifty Under Fifty, which wasn't true of some of the members anymore, but it was for Allison, who was forty and had published two novels and a collection of short fiction. In her mind she was tied among the Deep South graduates with Maya Drake, who had a great writer's name and though she only had two books, one had been a best-seller, briefly, and she also had a story in *The New Yorker*.

Allison was extremely jealous of Maya's literary agent, who had visited the Deep South Writer's Workshop their last year there, and she and Maya both had stories up that week, by design of the famous writer, but it was Maya's story the agent had come away impressed with. Allison didn't think Maya cared too much and never saw it as a competition. Allison knew she should have workshopped one of her old standby stories, like "The Existential Egg Salad," or "The Saddest Motel." Instead she had handed in something new, and she buckled under the pressure, because like everyone had said she didn't take any risks, her story about a graduate student in Mississippi no less, and so it was Maya who came away with accolades, for what was probably still her best story, the one about the family who threw a pool party three years after their teenaged daughter had drowned in the same pool. They were ready to live again, and it was incredibly awkward for everyone who had come to their pool party, but what were they going to do, tell this poor old couple and their remaining daughter they had something else that weekend and couldn't come? And once they were there the expectation was that everyone would swim and pretend to have a good time. The ghost of the dead girl was at the party too, and that was the masterstroke, according to the agent, because magic realism was hot that year.

Trent's email laid out what he'd heard from the famous writer's administrative assistant on the phone and Allison had to fight the urge to immediately take to Twitter to announce what she knew because it would result in a thousand retweets and there was no rush quite like a thousand retweets.

She carried her laptop over to her workspace, where her husband, Scott, had learned to leave her alone, because it was where she did her writing. He assumed she was in the grip of inspiration and would stay quiet on the other side of the room. She did so only so she wouldn't have to explain about Trent again. How she felt sorry for him because he tried so hard, but he couldn't get his sentences to break through. He was funny. He was imaginative. But that name. No one would ever buy a book from someone named Trent Sanivaugh.

She typed out an email to him, which she worked over to get just right, because she had the suspicion the email could end up, decades from now, in her archives or her published letters.

Dearest Trent,

Thank you for thinking of me and letting me know

about this dire news concerning our old friend. I wonder where I'd be today without Deep South. I'd be writing, for sure. But would my books, especially my debut, have been what they were? He had a hand in that. He guided us. He wasn't always kind about it, but I for one value honesty and the thick skins we developed that are so valuable, because even now, with all the success I've had, I still get rejections. I haven't had a NYer story yet. I haven't gotten a Pushcart. I suppose I'm more of a novelist than a story writer, but the foundation we developed as story writers, there's no substitute for that. I mean, maybe I'd have eventually gotten into Iowa, but there's no way to know for sure, and I'm glad it all happened the way it did.

And now what do we do? I feel like we all need to go see him. Who else are you in touch with? I can email Maya. She's easy enough to contact. But who else have you told? If Lydia says he wants to hear from us, certainly it's better to go see him. Tell me what you think? Someone could register with one of those high school reunion websites and we could plan a party. It would only be good if everyone could come. What do you think? Are you in? I am. I know it would be good to see you again. We keep in touch and all, but when was the last time we actually saw each other?

Are you writing? Of course you are. I'm in a slump and I may have time to look at a draft if you're ready. I know I'm not your ideal reader but I'll tell you what you need to hear.

All best,

A.

As soon as she sent the email she was kicking herself for say-ing she'd look at a manuscript. For all she knew he would send her a thousand pages he wanted feedback on. But she was afraid Trent would read some kind of romantic intention into her expressed de-sire to want to see him, so she added the part about feedback to keep it business-like. They had had one awkward date back in Petal. He had asked her out and she didn't think much of it, but he'd come on too strong, so she ended it right away. All these years later she believed he'd never gotten over her. He'd married but divorced and these days he never mentioned a girlfriend in his emails. For her-self, Allison was hopelessly devoted to Scott. They complimented each other precisely because they were different. She couldn't com-prehend his corporate legal and tax work and she would smile but zone out anytime he tried to talk about it. She liked to talk to him about the Titans or the Predators because they covered them con-stantly on the local news and 10:00 PM was pretty much their guar-anteed together time and the three-minute highlight reel was per-fect for giving her talking points on whether the Titans were having a winning season, or headed to the playoffs, or struggling with dis-appointing injuries, or if they'd made a promising trade. They had to sit through coverage of traffic accidents, home invasions, and mur-ders before her dose of local sports, but she would sometimes hold his hand on the sectional couch, or she'd lie down with her feet in his lap. There was no better time for wine, and they would have deep meaningful talks during the high school highlights and the com-mercials. She had tried to recreate those scenes, to get that feeling on the page, but words failed her in her connection with Scott. She was going to have to bring him to this reunion, she knew. He was jealous of any of her male writer friends and Scott also knew about the awkward date with Trent. She felt bad because she had made Trent sound more pathetic than he really was, and now it seemed Scott and Trent would finally meet. Scott could form his own opinion, and Scott tended to like people, especially anyone as genuine and kind as Trent.

Allison realized, as she thought this, that maybe she did have feelings for Trent, even still. If she were honest with herself the main reason she didn't date him while they were at Deep South was that she didn't want the other writers to see her as part of a couple. She needed to be independent, represented, in their minds, solely by her unique body of work. And while she could hardly admit this to herself, she had probably made an unnecessary sacrifice and she and Trent could have really helped each other, if she'd only let it happen. She understood now, that while she loved her husband, maybe there really was a danger of infidelity if she were to find herself alone with Trent for an extended period of time. And so she was glad she'd be bringing Scott, and she would try to be patient with his jealousies, because it had to be hard being the only non-creative person in the room. To be unread among those who were very well read. To be mostly devoid of curiosity and to have spent decades with tax law.

Allison walked barefoot across the new beige carpet, in lavender satin pajamas and with a glass of white wine. She sat next to Scott on the couch as he watched a football game that had gone late—not the Titans, she didn't know these teams—and she leaned into him and kissed him on the ear.

She said, "You're a good man, Scott," and she really meant it.

He had made the best of his rational sensibilities and pragmatic outlook and had provided splendidly for her. It was hard to admit that her writing, though critically acclaimed, didn't bring in much of anything. And thank God for the acclaim. Because without the national spotlight that she occasionally, however briefly, found herself in, she could be accused of being a fraud, a feminist who stayed home every day and let her husband control the finances. But with her name on the spine of three books, two from Harcourt Brace Jovanavich, she was an artist and a very good one at that. She understood the complexity of human relations and she was able to weave the English language, the greatest language, in the service of her vision.

§

Lydia knew that Maya Drake and the famous writer had stayed in contact, but she passed the lie along so that she might get Maya to increase the frequency of her correspondence. It was harder to lie to Maya, though, because she asked questions, she picked up on the tenor of Lydia's vocal quirks and got the feeling Lydia had fed her bullshit.

"I think he would have told me," Maya told Lydia. "Maybe you've misunderstood the seriousness. Maybe he's playing a joke on you."

Lydia agreed that he was capable of such a cruel prank, and it forced her to give Maya something more specific, which could unravel the whole endeavor if she said the wrong thing. She Googled cancer looking for something technical, while Maya remained skeptical. Lydia had bone, brain, or pancreas cancer in mind, and she couldn't decide which would best serve her, so she said, "It's in his heart. He only has six months to live."

"Heart cancer?"

"Not cancer. Not in. Like kind of. And near."

"He has a cancer-like condition near his heart?"

"There's a name for it," Lydia said. "I never remember."

"I don't know what you're up to," Maya said. "But if this is just a way to get us all together, there are better ways of going about it. I already got an email from Allison Avett and she's planned a reunion. If this is some kind of Andy Kaufmann thing he's trying to pull off you'd best tell him it's not funny. Everyone knows someone who has died of cancer. It happened to a character in my last book. I researched it pretty thoroughly and it will test your faith. He's an atheist so he probably doesn't give a shit, but it's not something to joke about."

"She's planned a reunion?"

"Allison didn't tell you?"

"I should be in the loop on that."

"Don't tell her I told you," Maya said.

"Don't tell anyone he's dying."

"See that's another thing. This is all very suspicious. I would think he would *enjoy* the attention if this were his last go-round. He'd fucking milk all the publicity out of it he could. He'd angle for a paperback deal to get his back catalog re-released."

And for the first time Lydia felt the weight of her lie, though it was too late to turn back.

She said, "Teaching was everything for him. You've all gone off and he wants to connect. Is that so wrong?"

"He had *better* be dying."

§

Trent did have a girlfriend, and while she was probably the best thing to ever happen to him, he was also looking forward to spending a weekend away without her. Because he couldn't bring her, because there would be drinking, a lot of drinking, and he would want to drink too, and after his girlfriend made the umpteenth comment about someone's being too drunk, some old friend of Trent's who he'd gotten drunk with many a time, he would start to think less of his girlfriend and he didn't want that. When they first started dating and she told him about being seven years sober, she had also said that if he drank in moderation it wasn't a problem, but her idea of moderation was different than his. If he only had one drink but never missed a day, was that moderation? If he had two drinks and never missed a day, was that moderation? If he didn't drink at all for three weeks and then got stinking drunk, was that moderation? In Trent's mind moderation was something like four drinks on any day that he felt like, sometimes more, sometimes not at all, and he liked a good spliff, though he didn't have a pot dealer and he knew if he ever brought it up that would mean splitsville with his girlfriend. She was smart enough to know that pot wasn't as bad as alcohol, but she had a troubling respect for the law that would cause him problems, so she definitely wasn't going, because maybe he'd get lucky and there'd be spliffs at this reunion party. Since she tended to give him shit over even the slightest version of moderate drinking, he had found it best to quit drinking around her entirely, without announcing it, so he could go back from time to time without being seen as a failure, at least to himself, which mattered, because when it came to his writing, he had been pretty hard on himself and had very keenly felt the successes of his peers while his own successes were far and few between. When he gave Allison Avett a manuscript, for example, he had thought maybe at least on a subconscious level she would see that he had surpassed her, but no, she was still churning out the same sentimental crap, and *The New York Times* and *Publishers Weekly* loved Allison Avett, and that was the position from which she critiqued his writing, sometimes ruthlessly, and that was another reason Trent's girlfriend would not be going, because he had read her some of Allison's critiques and his girlfriend, who was a fan of *Harry Potter* but otherwise not a reader, loved everything he had ever written and so she took Allison's biting critiques personally and she would hate-read each new book of Allison's. His girlfriend saw her as a shallow person, which Trent had to admit she kind of was, and there was no way he was going to facilitate those two ever being in a room together, so he never mentioned the existence of his girlfriend to Allison, who he was pretty sure thought he was madly in love with her because of that awkward date of theirs so many years ago, and Allison also always made a point to bring up her husband, the lawyer.

While it was charming that Trent's girlfriend loved everything he wrote, he also longed for someone he could swap manuscripts with who wasn't Allison. Her unsympathetic and unfair critiques of his work made him more sure of what he was doing, because he had an eye for nuances she couldn't see, but it also made him understand how hopeless it was, because if she was unable to recognize the value of what he was doing, he shouldn't expect anyone else to either. In fact, he should expect the opposite. Allison told him as much, though for different reasons, since she wholeheartedly believed in the value of what she was doing, which he was quite sure was drivel, overwritten and nearly plotless. It's main appeal to the literary establishment was that her writing was by, about, and for women, with a well-oiled marketing machine behind her to get her paperbacks out on the beaches and on the front tables at every

Barnes & Noble.

He knew Maya Drake was much too busy to look at his work, but she was the successful one who seemed to deserve her success. She didn't care about trends and she could tell a good story. But she was much too busy for him. Of course she was much too busy. She taught at Pitt. She reviewed books for *Slate*. She was sought after as a judge for writing contests and she also taught at two writers retreats each year, one in Portugal, and one in upstate New York.

Trent knew Maya would be a great reader for him, and if he could convince her to take a look at what he'd done lately, she'd appreciate the turns. She might not recommend him to her literary agent, but she'd respect what he'd done and understand how lucky she'd been, that on that workshop day all those years ago when her agent first met her, she'd been the one to hand in the better story, while Allison's was uninspired. Trent didn't harbor any resentment toward the famous writer for setting up the agent's visit for Allison and Maya, because like Allison, he wasn't ready for that then. He was now. He'd had to work for it, in obscurity, but he'd arrived. It was conceited to say, maybe, but he knew he was the best writer out of the bunch, even if no one else would ever understand that.

As that thought lingered an idea blossomed in him that he knew he could finally make happen. The reunion wasn't simply an opportunity for them to get together, but they could workshop. The famous writer, in his last days, could be surrounded by his best and most successful students, many of whom had gone out and made good, and he could lead one last all-star workshop. The idea was so good he emailed Allison immediately. Their nickname for the famous writer had been Mr. Kurtz, after the character from *Heart of Darkness*, the colonial colonel who mastered over the African natives even as he lay dying. Trent remembered that the famous writer really was dying, and this last workshop might not be too far from the sweaty muttering mad Apocalypse *Now* performance of Marlon Brando as he expounded on "the horror" to his assassin in a jungle in Vietnam. He tried to put it out of his mind, afraid that the famous writer, who was often too direct in his dismantling of their writing, might be even less kind to them as Death hovered near. Whatever they had written and whatever they had done with their lives, he could cut with a searing utterance. They'd gotten out of his grip, but he was in their heads, and as absurd as it seemed, they still longed for his approval.

Hey Alli,

I was thinking about this reunion. I'm totally on board. I think it might be fun for us to workshop. I mean when else would we get the chance? Do you think Kurtz would be up for it? It should be perfectly natural for him. It's how he knew us and how we interacted. Heck, who knows? He might even be nice.

T

Trent,

Let me mull it over. I'm not sure "fun" is the right word. You may be a masochist.

Alli

But Alli was also on board. She didn't know what story to workshop, but the idea of going up against Maya Drake for a re-do was appealing to her. She also craved the seal of approval from their old mentor, who was familiar with her body of work as it had grown, and developed, and been written about in the *New York Times*. Lydia could set it up, and unless the famous writer objected for some reason that she couldn't fathom, the last workshop could happen.

§

The famous writer went about his Wednesday unaware that people thought he was dying. He'd told his secretary to reach out to his former students, and he had the impression that this reaching out had worked, nothing more and nothing less, because he was getting lots of emails all of a sudden. Not only did they write and tell him about their lives since graduation, but several of them seemed to want to visit, which he wasn't sure he wanted, though he supposed it was nice, and one or two of them had this idea that instead of a party, the focus should be a writing workshop, which, if he was honest, given the number of former-students involved, would be a marathon workshop, and frankly, he thought it was weird. He had merely wanted to hear from them and instead they wanted a piece of him and they were willing to come all that way to make work for him. To read a story from everyone and talk about it for an afternoon—obviously they didn't remember how exhausting that was. The central experience of old age for him had been that it made one more tired, and his response was to become—justifiably—more lazy. There were times in recent years that he would go to a workshop without having read the stories and he found he could still fill the class time. He would let the students do all the talking until he found a point of entry to talk about movies. He went to the movies at least once a week. He'd go more often, but this was Mississippi, and his choices were limited.

There would be a discussion about a story, a question about the authenticity of the narrative voice, and the famous writer would pop in with: "You know, I hate it when a movie has a narrator. There's this guy talking over the film. Who is this guy? Why is he there? Who is he supposed to be talking to?"

These were questions he didn't really want answered and if one of the students tried, he'd bite her head off.

"What I like to do," he said, "when I'm watching a movie at home. I watch with the sound all the way down."

"Muted?"

"No," he said, "not muted. Because then you get that little 'mute icon in the corner of the screen and it ruins the cinematography, but with the sound turned all the way down. Anybody else do that?"

Two or three suck-ups raised a hand. He noted who they were and nodded his approval. He would remember to be nicer to them from then on since they understood the importance of silence in the narrative arts, though they would also hand in stories with yammering narrators.

"There's all this talk-talk-talking," he said. "Nobody wants to read talking."

"How do I get ideas across, I wonder," the writer of the piece said, breaking protocol, but so exasperated at the ridiculous direction the discussion had taken that he couldn't help it.

The famous writer waved a finger at him, to reinforce the rule that the writer could only speak at the beginning and the end of the workshop. As long as they were discussing the story, he had to sit there, quietly, and take it.

"What I want," the famous writer said, "is a story without a narrator."

"No narrator?" the writer being workshopped said, and he threw up his arms.

"Like 'Hills Like White Elephants'?" one of the suck-ups offered.

"*No!* not like 'Hills Like White Elephants'!" the famous writer shouted. "I'm so sick of that story. The abortion should have been Hemingway, so we'd never again have to read that story."

"It's a good story," the writer being workshopped said, and he looked directly at the famous writer when he said it, so that what was inferred was, "better than any of yours."

There was a long silence that was only broken when one of the suck-ups said, "I hated 'Hills' too."

"'Hate' is a little strong, don't you think?" the writer being workshopped said.

"Okay, I don't *hate* it," the famous writer said, and he added, "but you really need to stop talking."

The writer being workshopped made the zipped-lips gesture and a productive discussion continued until the famous writer got bored and decided he wanted to talk about movies again, with Cohen Brothers movies easily the most discussed flicks of his workshops, and he went there now, saying something about the brilliance of Clooney, which was hard to argue with, but also completely irrelevant. The suck-ups added a few of their own Cohens-Brothers-related observations to run out the clock, and he'd made it through once again without reading the story, with no one the wiser.

As he walked to his MG, he remembered the proposed reunion and the idea of having all these extra stories to read, from well-published writers who, some of them, ran workshops of their own now, which was a little terrifying. Until he remembered that he was the famous writer, and he welcomed the challenge. He'd take good notes. He'd slack off on his classes in order to free up time. He'd cut back on movie-watching. It would be a lot of stories to read and respond to, but he'd somehow started this whole thing.

§

Despite a good first couple of days of getting in touch with former students, Lydia had hit a wall. Once the application process was made electronic, she lost access. The applications had been emailed in, and the university email archive hadn't been large enough to continue to keep them, so applications were arbitrarily deleted after a certain date. There were the most recent students, who she still had contact information for, and the ones from way back, fifteen years or more ago when the applications were mailed in on paper, with nothing in between. And there among the paper applications was a name she recognized with no need to call, because the student had dropped out to become the famous writer's girlfriend. Lydia wasn't working here then and could only imagine the murmurs this had caused. Though maybe it hadn't. Because maybe this kind of thing was seen as normal then. The young woman still lived in Petal, in an apartment complex near campus, where she resided as the famous writer's long-term girlfriend.

So this reunion was going to be the students who had graduated in the most recent years and the ones who had been gone for twenty. She supposed they would bond over their shared experiences with the famous writer and with living in Petal, but it was looking to be a group of the starry-eyed alongside the seasoned and cynical. She wasn't sure how well the older ones would mix, and she hoped, if they persisted in this workshop idea, that they would segregate themselves by year of attendance. But when she ran the idea by her boss, he looked at her as if she should have known that any idea that created more work for him was a bad idea, no matter how well-intentioned or sensible.

"It doesn't matter if they get along," he said. "Why do they have to get along?"

§

The ones who had known the famous writer in recent years weren't as affected by the news of his terminal illness and they were perplexed by the idea that some had wanted to get together to workshop. They hadn't been gone long enough to idealize the famous writer and their idea of how to break through as a writer had more to do with online branding than attention to words, which could become pathological, and that kind of tinkering, theoretically at least, had no end point. Their nickname for the famous writer was Bobby Knight, who they were all too young to experience in action, but they had YouTube and every group of writers came with a sports nerd or two, so the allusion wasn't lost on them and easily explained, Bobby Knight a notoriously cruel coach.

One of the writers in this group was a kid named Jeremy who, among a certain circle of younger writers, was recognized as "Internet famous" under the moniker iMOL. It had been his gamer tag and when he handed in stories at Deep South, his iMOL persona seemed closer to what he'd intended with the work than what his life had added up to as Jeremy, and so once he started handing in stories as iMOL, and publishing as iMOL, there was this online presence of extreme contemporaneity that he had constructed, and he was iMOL. Bobby Knight was sometimes amused at the ways this new batch of kids handed in stories formatted to look like conversations on Facebook, and while he explained there would be copyright issues, none of them cared a whit about that and two weeks later the piece would be published on some online magazine out of Brooklyn, with none of the suggestions made by fellow writers during workshop reflected in the final piece.

As soon as he got off the phone with Lydia, iMOL sent a Google Hangouts invite to FeministaFittySent, who didn't publish under that name, but stuck with Trisha, though she abbreviated her last name as the byline for the radical reactions to each new pop culture bubble she published at any aggregate blog that would have her, and she was Trisha A. She appeared on iMOL's laptop and soon enough they were talking, as they often did, as if they had never left Mississippi though they lived across the country from each other, FeministaFittySent in New York City, obviously, and iMOL in Nebraska where he was from.

"What do they want from him?" Trisha A. said.

"Who knows?" iMOL said. "I looked up as many as I could from their email addresses. They're pretty old school. I mean *Alaska Quarterly* is impressive, I guess, but who has time for that? And like, I look at the covers and all I can think is that magazine will put me to sleep."

"Some of them, you can't even find their work online," Trisha A. said. "So like, what's the point?"

"There are people who took Bobby Knight's classes before the Internet."

"Shut up. The Internet was invented in 1991. There's nobody older than that."

"He was teaching before that," iMOL said. "For like, a long time."

"So if we go to this workshop are we going to read stories with payphones and shit?"

"I don't know. Maybe. They want to start a Facebook group. They at least know how to do that."

"Facebook is boring."

"You wrote a story with Facebook in it," iMOL said.

"Like six years ago or something. I've moved on."

"Yeah, me too. Do you want to go to this thing? Fuck an old married guy or something?"

"You can. Maybe I will go, though. To tell Bobby Knight not to go gentle into that good night."

"I think it would be 'to not go gentle'."

"No, that's split infinitive."

"Is it?"

"The line is 'do not go gentle,' but it's hard to get 'do' into the sentence I used."

"Why aren't you an editor?"

"I am. At *Fembot Occlusion*."

"Right," iMOL said. "I forget because I can't send you anything."

"We publish dudes."

"Self-castrating submissive dudes."

"Is that what you think?" Trisha A. said. "There happens to be some great feminist fiction coming from writers who just happen to be male-bodied."

"Like one in two hundred."

"It's more than that."

"Not a lot more."

"Send us that piece about your mom."

"I can't," iMOL said. "She started following me on Tumblr."

"Oh God, no."

"I know."

"What does she say?"

"What *can* she say? She focuses on the one part she understands and says that was really good, even if it was something I intended ironically, or it was put there as an iconoclastic bit of absurd nonsense. But you can't tell her that."

"Just say, 'Thanks!'" Trisha A. said.

"Exactly."

"She did pay your tuition."

"I worked," iMOL objected.

"To pay for beer and weed."

"That was part of it."

"They mean well."

"I can't think too much about it, but there's no way I'm sending that piece to *Fembot Occlusion*."

"Write something else."

"Like what?"

"We've got a theme issue coming up."

"I hesitate to ask."

"No, it's good. *Feminine Mystique* 53 years later."

"You missed the 50?" iMOL said.

"We missed the 50. But it's still good. You can do whatever you want: a monologue, a satire, a lyric essay."

"It *is* a good book."

"It's a *great* book."

"I'll meditate on it."

"So are you going to this thing?"

"Yeah," iMOL said. "I think I have to. I could get like six blog posts out of it."

"Me too," Trisha A. said. "I was thinking the exact same thing."

§

The chancellor of the university and the provost were in the back of the chancellor's wife's Mercedes, with the air conditioning blasting, as his student intern drove them up to the rose garden in front of Alumni Hall, the most iconic building on campus, with the dome and the bell tower, and four groundskeepers tending to the rose bushes. The chancellor rolled down his window and shouted at the grounds manager, "Ready by spring break, Al?"

Al held up his fists to indicate the anticipated size of the blooms by then, "They'll be this big!"

"Perfect," the chancellor said, and he rolled his window back up. From spring break to the end of the year was when they had the most prospective students visit with their parents, and the mothers always loved the rose garden. Winning over mothers was the key to the next year's enrollment. There was nothing quite like a mature and well-tended rose garden to make those parents feel good about spending tuition dollars, and they sat parked in the Mercedes a while longer to watch the men work.

The provost was reminded of something and he perked up, "There are some alumni planning a reunion of sorts over spring break."

"Oh?"

"The rumor is that the head of our writing program has a terminal illness, and so this a great opportunity for us to get out front in front of hiring."

"A director?"

"A writer. A famous writer."

"Like Dean Koontz? Someone like that?"

"Not quite that famous. Ideally, it would be someone young who had won an award."

"Like a Pulitzer?"

"Not a Pulitzer. Maybe a finalist for a Pulitzer. We want name recognition but someone who also needs a job."

"I see. What are those books all the kids are reading?"

"*Harry Potter*?"

"No, the other one."

"..."

"Who am I thinking of," the chancellor asked the intern.

"*Hunger Games*?" the intern said.

"*That's* it. We get the *Hunger Games* guy."

"She's a woman, and still too famous."

"We could poll the students. Send out one of them Survey Chimps."

"Our writer hasn't died yet, so we can't do that."

"Have you got any ideas?"

"I don't have a list or anything," the provost said. "I was thinking a woman, probably black, maybe Latina, or Hawaiian. Or you know, lesbian."

"We can't get the *Hunger Games* guy, but we can find a semi-famous black lesbian Latina?"

"I think we probably could."

"That would look good?"

"We've had this white guy running things since the seventies. I think it would look great."

"We'd get more applications?"

"Probably the same number of applications."

"But it would look good."

"It would look great."

"Who do we put on this? Who do we know who reads?"

"We need to keep it hush-hush until we can actually make an offer. But we can Google around and make initial contact, try to gauge interest, that sort of thing."

"And these black lesbian Latinas would want to move to Mississippi?"

"They would want to run the Deep South Workshop."

"Is that what we call it? Has a nice ring, don't you think?"

"It does. And we'd be updating it."

"Nothing ironic about that?"

"Nothing at all."

§

Over the weeks since he'd corresponded with Allison Avett, Trent Sanivaugh skimmed his five novel manuscripts looking for something to excerpt that he could hand in as a story for the reunion workshop. He had built elaborate verbal structures and he had smart lovable characters, with some perfect scenes, but they didn't hold up well outside the context of the novel, and this was true time after time, and so he was going to have to write a brand new short story, but about what?

Write what you know. Trent knew from a young age that money inspired people to do dumb things, sometimes at great cost. He remembered a patch of woods surrounded by gas stations and stores, so it was only a matter of time before someone razed the small woods to create more of the same, but when the trees were cut down, the muddy lot was put up for sale, and it stayed that way, for years and years, the wreckage of a large square of land with bulldozer tracks and piles of rubbish, water erosion and patches of wild grass. Someone had made money but lacked the foresight to make something useful, and the only green that remained on that side of town were the strips of lawn that outlined parking lots.

Trent knew the best way to make friends, as an adult, was to compliment other adults on their children. He knew there was some kind of invisible stranglehold over most of the world that allowed him to buy cheap t-shirts and sign up for a free cell phone, but also that there were better places than Georgia, for workers' rights, for health care, for education. Trent worked as a high school English teacher for six years, until he was pulled over, the cop tore his car apart, and found one of his spliffs. It wasn't a felony, but it was in the paper, a paper his principal religiously read. Trent was allowed to finish out the year, for everyone else's convenience, and then he'd never get another teaching job again. It was just as well. The students he liked best were the ones who didn't give a shit, and he didn't gleam the adult version of school spirit and he was too well educated to teach from the required textbook, which was terrible. His principal seemed relieved to have finally caught Trent and to be able to let him go. He suggested that any ruinous cascade of events that was to come was directly the result of Trent's own folly.

From then on, Trent knew the value of a dollar. He knew the impermanence of gainful employment and the arbitrary value systems exercised within. He knew that no amount of hard work would reward him for spending his life writing the way that it had Allison

Avett, and he knew that she felt she deserved every lucky break she got.

But what kind of story would he write? He needed a setting, he needed a character as unlike himself as possible, and he needed a plot. What plot would best communicate his hard-won wisdom? What plot would stand against the entropy of time? He thought of the great canon of Western literature, of all stories he loved, and he mulled them over for ways to update them, to copy them, to move them in new directions, to unravel them, to put two of them together, to switch the gender of the characters, or to choose a new point of view character. And what could he possibly write to touch his fellow inhabitants of twenty-first-century late consumerist capitalism, who suffered from a century without God and who were fatigued from instant entertainments, each more immediate and visceral? Something weighty? Something funny? Something true?

He sat with the laptop in his studio apartment above the flower shop, and their bell chimed with each customer coming and going. The desire for flowers was easily fulfilled with flowers. And it was a great apartment because the florist closed at six and from then on he was free to be as loud as he wanted, which mostly meant turning up The White Stripes, or The Strokes, or The Clash, because by then he would have written as much as he could hope to, and despite whatever dumb job he might go to that night or that weekend, he'd worked another day toward self-fulfillment, and even if his current labors went unpublished, he knew the value of his talents, and this self-knowledge lifted him up.

He thought about the teenage ghost girl from Maya Drake's story from so long ago. The way her parents had persisted in throwing a pool party, as years had passed and she was frozen in photographs, on the verge of, but never becoming an adult. She passed through walls and wandered from room to room, and as Trent understood the allure of the story it wasn't so much that magic realism was hot that year, but that Maya had captured the angsty boredom of the teenager trapped in the suburban nuclear family. Her inability to ever leave that space was the source of so much pathos that the parents had tried to exorcise by throwing a party that their neighbors and friends were captive to, if only for a night.

He imagined what it might have been like for the girl to have been brought back to life and he was reminded of the pain of Lazarus. There was an old Russian story, one of his favorites, that ended with the townspeople confronting Lazarus., "Tell us what you've seen!" And without answer or description or Biblical allusion, the reader knows the landscape of the underworld is unspeakable, and inhabiting it wrecks comfort and reason.

Nature too can show us such wild indifference. And he imagined his teenage girl lost in the woods but brought back, only the town was different, and her home was gone. She would be adopted by new parents and would do her best to get to know them, and to love, and be loved, but she would never again feel connected. She would be a good girl, afraid of causing trouble, but would wander this life detached, with no value on the rewards, unable to self-delude, the unspeakable always right below the surface. What can the adoptive parents do with such a morose child? How will the world accept one prone to uttering unsugared truths?

By the time the florist closed, Trent had two sentences, all he would get today because he had to shower before putting on his stupid uniform to serve jalapeño poppers and domestic drafts in frozen mugs: "Joan followed the path into the woods. She had been there yesterday with a boy who knew the trails, and she hoped to retrieve her lost locket."

§

The day the National Book Award finalists were announced, there was a flurry of activity on the Deep South Writers Reunion Facebook group that Allison Avett had started. They bonded over the books they had read, lamented that they hadn't read them all, and rooted for the personality they liked best. These writers had all won, obviously, since getting this recognition was huge in terms of sales and their ability to continue to publish. There were five finalists: three white women in their mid-thirties who went to Iowa or Michigan and moved to New York, one stalwart older than Kurtz/Bobby Knight, and a young debut story writer who was a bisexual half-Chinese Dominican granddaughter of the current Australian Ambassador to the Dominican Republic. Despite her book being a collection of stories, and the unevenness of her work, easily attributed to shooting-star-status finding her much too young for the company they placed her with, her unique point of view made her the Deep South favorite, with the white mid-thirties Brooklynite who had published on the hip small press a close second. This hip small press was unsuccessfully trying to fulfill orders and it was evident that her book was going to be bought out by one of the "big five" publishing house/media conglomerates, and that would delay the re-release of her book, going from a paperback with a well-designed but cheap cover to a hardback edition with the gold seal on the jacket that declared her a "National Book Award Finalist."

On the Deep South Writers Facebook group Maya Drake wrote a short post where she stuck up for the old white guy. Sure, he was doing what he'd always done, but he was really, really good at it, and none of the other finalists could touch his sentences. Or his plots. Or his characters. Maya believed he was easily the best writer of the bunch, with the best book, but also that he would lose, because the book world was clamoring for something new.

Allison had only read one of the books, because her literary agent also represented that other white woman in her thirties and had wanted Allison to blurb it. The book was highly anticipated but the least interesting of the finalists, as the least literary, so that it had no chance of winning, but it had been optioned and was already in pre-production with Terrence Malick and Amy Adams attached. Allison couldn't really bring herself to read the book. She liked what she had skimmed well enough, but her task was to write a sentence or two to pitch it to the undecided reader who had picked it up off of the storefront table. She focused more on the writer than this particular book, and had said, "Martha Mueller's work resonates with the uncommon wonder of histories brought to life with the wit and clarity of a master story-teller." As the anticipation grew, her blurb got bumped off the final jacket copy, but they did put her vague exaggerated pitch up at the author's website, where it was crowded out by the comments of twenty other writers, fifteen of whom were easily more famous than Allison. She felt like she'd wasted her time. She didn't even like that book, but she also wondered if anyone at the Deep South Facebook group had seen her blurb—she doubted it—and it put her in the position of having a sense of loyalty to Martha Mueller. They shared a literary agent, after all. Of all the finalists, if Martha Mueller could get in, it gave Allison hope that one day that gold seal and the twenty blurbs would go on a book of her own.

Of course Trent had something negative to say about all of the finalists, and he'd killed the discussion. The Deep South Facebook group went quiet after that for weeks, even after the young bisexual Chinese Dominican was awarded the prize and American literati of mostly upper-class white women readers heralded the minuscule victory her win represented as a pushback against the Western patriarchal hegemony.

The provost and the chancellor lamented that she had won, because it put her out of reach as a replacement for the famous writer, and their short list of nonwhite lesbian writers had gotten shorter. They were beginning to realize they would wind up with one of the Iowa graduates living in New York, who were hetero, and who had lifestyles that would make it next to impossible to convince them to move to Petal, Mississippi. But there were still gay men, and hetero women of color. They would find a suitable writer, there was no doubt about it. If anything, the announcement of the National Book Award winner reassured them they were on the right track.

§

When Allison Avett discovered that the National Book Award winner and the famous writer shared the same literary agent she embarked on something she wasn't proud of, but that she felt she had no choice pursuing. More than anything, she was sure the National Book Award winner would currently be toiling away in Chinese Dominican obscurity if not for this powerful force of an agent, and Allison devised to use the famous writer's terminal illness as a way to invite this agent to the reunion. It used to be that literary agents worked behind the scenes and no one ever knew who they were. In the age of social media, the writers who sought an agent had access to knowledge about them. Literary agents tweeted snark about the mountain of manuscripts the wannabe writers continued to send them, despite their clearly stated no-open-submission policies.

The famous writer's agent, Austin Goldman, had been inaccessible since long before Allison had tried to write. The air of exclusivity he evoked was one way to insure his writers got great deals. This meant one could never find their way to him through hard work. Generally, another agent recognized a shooting star shortly before he did, but if he saw something bankable, which was pretty much guaranteed as the direct result of his representation, then he'd claim ownership and immediately raise the value of the property. He had an aura of success that he fed by wearing white suits and by taking his lunch meetings at the most expensive restaurants in the city, that publishers paid for, and where he would never eat or drink until he got a verbal agreement, with the most enticing dishes ever plated congealed and cold in front of him as he stonewalled until the editor surrendered to his terms, most often before the editor had read the full manuscript. So many deals were made on the opening pages of a novel that Goldman had built an empire on them. It didn't matter if the book was any good, so long as it had buzz. He'd pit an editor from one publishing house against a rival and they'd be topping each other's offers for a book that could never pay out, and two years later these same editors would be working for different publishing houses, and he'd do the same to them again with another hot writer they just couldn't bear to say 'no' to.

And Allison knew, if she could just get in the room with Goldman, she could hand him a stack of opening pages that would knock his argyle socks off. Yes, she already had an agent, an agent she owed her writing career to, but who would understand, since this was the business. When she thought about it more, she was sure her literary agent wouldn't understand. They'd spent a Thanksgiving together. Her agent picked up Allison when she was first getting started and she had the covers of all of Allison's books prominently featured on her website, even though she'd picked up more than a few best-selling authors since then. Really, it didn't matter. Allison's fantasy was stupid because Goldman would never be interested in a writer who'd been marketed in women's magazines as a "beach read." If there was one thing Allison Avett absolutely did not have, it was buzz. And Goldman would sense that about her immediately.

She was in a very good place compared to the other Deep South graduates, but she wasn't satisfied. She could go on Goodreads and see that more than 350 people had read her last book and left positive comments, but it wasn't satisfying. *Publishers Weekly* had given her starred reviews, but it wasn't enough. Mostly, her emotional fulfillment came by avoiding the unimaginable. How would she get out of bed in the morning if she *didn't* get a starred review, or how would she continue to commit sentences to the virtual paper of MS Word if 350 people wrote *negative* comments about her books? And how in the hell did Trent continue to do what he did with no recognition at all? She hesitated to call it courage because she saw Trent's stubborn refusal to see the light as something akin to stupidity, and even if she were in his position, she certainly wasn't stupid, and so maybe she'd give up, maybe she'd quit. This was unthinkable to her now, though in reality she hadn't written anything in three years. She had but she hadn't. She'd pursued ideas that didn't add up. She'd leapt into false starts but couldn't move on. So, yes, she had written over the past three years, but not with consistency and not anything anyone would ever read. Realizing it now made her so low she could hardly bring herself to email Goldman to invite him to the reunion. But then she decided that if she were given the chance to meet Goldman, and to pitch to him, then it would motivate her to write something great. She'd shown the potential, and now would be her time. Maya had had her time, the famous writer had had his, and now was her time. She was so sure of this she went to Goldman's website where he made it abundantly clear he didn't want to receive any emails from anyone other than industry professionals ready to make wild offers. But the terminal illness of one of his celebrated authors had to count as an exception. After a few stunted apologetic tries, Allison wrote to Goldman with the confidence of someone who deserved his attention. She hit the caps lock, and in the subject line of the email, she wrote, "URGENT!" She supposed that's how all of his correspondence came to him, but she knew he wouldn't recognize her name, and she believed this would get him to read her email.

Mr. Goldman,

I may be betraying my mentor, the famous writer, who doesn't want people to know, but he's dying. He's someone who has done so much for so many writers over the years, and he doesn't know but we're planning a reunion in his honor. Many of us have been away for years without keeping in contact, and we wanted to thank him for the time he spent fostering us as young artists. As his literary agent, and someone who has known him throughout his writing career, we wanted to be sure to extend this invitation for you as well. We haven't cemented a date, as of yet, but we are looking at spring break, at the end of March, when there will be very few people on campus and we can expect to have the run of the place. Should you decide to participate, you'd have a chance to say a few words and your appearance would be a surprise. Please don't let him know you're coming.

In addition, this might also be a fruitful visit for you. We've decided to have one last workshop. You'd be welcome to sit in, your opinion greatly valued, and who knows, you might discover new talent. At the very least, it should prove to be a memorable couple of days of wine and reminiscing.

Please respond at your convenience, so we know ahead of time whether or not we shall have the pleasure of your company.

Yours,

Allison A. Avett, Ph.D.

For the rest of the day she suffered over the email that she'd already sent and couldn't change. She knew the bit about new talent was reaching. And when did she ever sign emails with Ph.D.? She felt so stupid. She was sure she had approached him all wrong. She was sure he would never ever look at her work or represent her, and she was also sure he would not be coming.

She had a block of time reserved for writing but she fidgeted, snacked on yogurt and Triscuits, and kept returning to her email to look for a reply. Her writing time was ruined for the day and she'd also blown the possibility of ever working with Austin Goldman. She had a personal rule about drinking before 5:00 PM, but at 3:37 she uncorked a Chablis from the fridge and sat drinking as she scoured the Internet for low-heeled reasonable but expensive-looking sexy shoes. She filled her cart at one site, then moved on to the next.

As she reached the last third of the bottle of Chablis, she'd bought six pairs of nearly identical shoes from four online stores and had spent $800. She had managed not to think at all about Austin Goldman and how he could make her writing career entirely satisfying by simply doing what he did, but she would have to content herself with knowing that anytime she wanted, even in the middle of the night, she could buy sexy shoes.

§

When Goldman read Allison's email he shook his head and laughed. He could sense desperation in her suggestion that he attend their cute workshop, which was the last thing he'd ever want to do. He wasn't who he was because he guided writers through a *process*. He took the finished product and got the people who sold such things extremely excited about what he had that they suddenly wanted. He would rather die than spend an afternoon in a room of equally desperate writers so full of desire for that kind of success that they could hardly patch together a decent plot and would stick to what they'd come up with no matter how forcefully he explained their wrongheaded approach.

He remembered his old friend, and how the former student had said he was dying, and he supposed he owed him a phone call. He certainly wasn't the most famous writer in his stable, but Goldman had sold a lot of his books over the years, each less important than the one before, and Goldman was loyal if nothing else. Once he took a writer on he stuck with them, to prove there really was the buzz that he himself had created. Not one to mince words, Goldman got right to the heart of the matter.

Goldman: I received an email from some writer of yours. This girl who writes books about being divorced and going around Europe. Does this ring a bell?

FW: Avett.

Goldman: She's under the impression that you are dying.

FW: We are all dying.

Goldman: She painted a picture with more immediacy.

FW: She hasn't talked to me.

Goldman: In all my years I've never had a writer pull a ploy like that. It's disgusting.

FW: Take some credit. You bring it out in them.

Goldman: Have some decency. Accept mediocrity. There *are* other agents.

FW: She has an agent. Hence the Europe books.

Goldman: Are you lying to me? Does she have reason to believe what she seems to believe?

FW: I have no foreknowledge of my impending demise. Probably a rumor. They have started other rumors.

Goldman: About you sleeping with that girl. Which one was she. She didn't pan out, did she?

FW: The relationship or her career? No, she didn't. Though we did embed one another. Repeatedly.

Goldman: Spare me the details.

FW: Hazard of the job.

Goldman: If you are dying we can make use of this. Even if it's only a rumor I can get it out there and pretend I had nothing to do with it. I'm surprised we didn't think of this before.

FW: You reprimand the girl but would use the same rumor in much the same way?

Goldman: It's not the same. It's my job. She wanted clout. Which I don't dole out unearned.

FW: One has to earn the clout.

Goldman: They're planning some kind of get-together. They wanted me to come.

FW: How sweet. Now this is sounding like fun. You *should* come. We can make them suffer for it.

Goldman: I may. Are there still casinos down there?

FW: Just like old times.

Goldman: I'll pencil it in. By no means do you tell that girl, though. It'll take everything I have to avoid her.

FW: I don't doubt that you can shut her down in an instant. You're even looking forward to it.

Goldman: Someone's got to teach her.

FW: I tried. You can't beat it out of some of them. It's a truth universally acknowledged that everyone falls in love with their own shit.

§

That evening as the sun made its descent, the famous writer went to his writing workshop with a heavy heart. He had always been superstitious and this news out of the blue—from Austin Goldman of all people—that he was terminally ill, was not a good omen. He drove his MG with the top down an extra loop around the university drive without pulling into the usual parking lot because he wanted to experience the first lights of spring as shown by the diminished coverage of the wardrobe choices of the young women in flip-flops snapping along to and from class. He would miss all this, if he were to die, the grand history of the school represented by the iconic Alumni Hall and its cupola, the falafel place on the corner where they knew him and gave him twice the allotted portion of diced tomatoes, and the parade of beautiful hardly-dressed young women. He remembered then that he was an atheist and would have no experience of missing anything. It would all be black. Or not even that, an unknown unknowable black. No experience of anything or even an awareness what an experience was or had been. He'd be gone, zip, zero. But at least he'd said what he wanted in his books. Or good enough. Or not even that, but he was glad he'd written them, even if the critics weren't. Maybe they'd wake up to him once he was gone, though he doubted it, because he didn't even see all that much value in what he had written, at least not when confronted with the black unknown unknowable.

Finally, he parked. He contemplated making an appointment with his physician, to be on the safe side. And he cheered up somewhat as he walked toward Nathan Bedford Forrest Hall, where he'd held his workshops for decades, a humanities building like all humanities buildings: old and utilitarian, unattractive and either too hot or too drafty, with scattered unmatched desks, rooms that always had at least one flickering buzzing fluorescent light, and dusty wide aluminum blinds that tended not to work. They would sit around a wide conference table and he hadn't read the stories, but tonight at least he had a good excuse and he could make use of the rumor to direct the discussion back around to himself, and his legacy, which the suck-ups would know exactly how to defend, which he needed to hear, because someone out there was spreading the rumor that he was dying, and if he didn't find the silver lining, the weight could drag him down.

As always, he was late, and they'd been sitting around waiting for him. He'd forbidden them to talk about the stories to be work-shopped before he arrived, but he suspected they'd been doing just that. They all had guilty looks, especially the suck-ups, and so he chose to take whatever they'd been talking about head-on, and he opened with, "The news of my death has been greatly exaggerated."

They got the reference. If there was anything they were good at, it was catching these types of allusions, but they didn't get the context and so he'd started the workshop by creating an uncomfort-able air. This meant they certainly weren't the source of the rumor, these fourteen amateurs who came to him because they wanted to write. Their puzzled looks gave away that they hadn't yet heard.

"Someone's been saying that I'm sick and I'm going to die."

They looked at each other, shocked, and none of them knew what to say. One of the suck-ups took a shot, "But you're not, right?"

"I may be. I don't know."

That wasn't the response the suck-up had anticipated.

"Would you be interested in meeting graduates of the workshop?" the famous writer said. "Some of the writers from way back? From twenty years or so ago? They seem to want to workshop for some reason."

They had no interest in this at all. They liked each other well enough but throwing older writers into the mix with their own bag-gage seemed like more than any of them should have to put up with.

They were paying to be here, after all. Were these new/old writers going to show up and take workshop time for free? A few shrugged their shoulders because the famous writer waited for a response.

"My agent might also be coming. If we let this rumor run its course, you'll all get to meet the great Austin Goldman. How does that sound?"

They understood that what he offered was something exceptional, but none of them was ready as writers for what he'd meant to convey with that opportunity, especially the suck-ups, who were at least more socially inclined to take advantage of a situation like that. They looked at each other and shrugged their shoulders again.

"It could be fun," the famous writer said.

This was a word they'd learned not to trust coming from someone who had earned the nickname Bobby Knight, and they were mostly wishing that this proposed reunion would not happen, and that one of them would muster up the guts to say so.

"They want to do this over spring break," he said, and this lifted the mood in the room immediately. "I suppose some of you have plans."

Yes, yes, yes, they all had plans, and everyone in the room talked about going home for a week, or flying out to see a boyfriend, or hiking, or visiting kitschy tourist destinations to blog about, or they were going to L.A. or New York, because they were writers, and those creative crucibles were the natural habitats of writers, and they should start getting used to the air out there.

"Get your parents to come here," he suggested. "What's to see in New York?" he surmised, though he knew, and he wished he were the kind of writer to run a workshop there instead of here, though sleepy Mississippi had its undeniable charms, not the least of which was the brushing off of inappropriate teacher-student sexual rela-tionships. Not that it couldn't happen in New York or L.A, but he'd be far more likely to be sued or reprimanded and dragged down for it. Here, he only had to deal with his girlfriend, who had once been his student, and who refused to marry him despite his con-stant begging. He wasn't ready to be married. He had been married, twice, and had fucked up before, and there was no reason to believe he wouldn't again. Marriages could be open, he suggested. No, they could not, she told him in no uncertain terms, and she remained his girlfriend, who he saw mostly on weekends, though tonight he was sure to turn the rumor of his dying and the depression it stirred in him as a way of getting her to cheer him up with orgasms. The plu-ral was maybe too optimistic, but he was a writer, after all, and he had every intention of working toward the plural. This rumor was a first, and he didn't suspect he'd encounter the likes of it again.

This is where his mind was when the students talked about the stories they had written and handed in that week. He was able to follow that one story was about a dentist who had enacted some kind of scheme to get rich off of gold teeth that didn't make sense to him, and when there had been a lull in the discussion, he tried to make his overarching sense of disbelief known without revealing how little he knew about the story. The last thing he wanted was to have the writer blurt out, despite the no-talking-rule, that the scheme had been explained in plain prose on page two, exactly as he'd always told them to do. And so he gave off a negative vibe but danced around the details, and it worked, since one of the suck-ups recovered for him.

"He goes through dental school," the suck-up said, "and he sup-ports his dentistry practice, with several people working for him and all this expensive equipment—and he's going to get rich on gold teeth? It doesn't make sense."

"I for one was able to suspend my disbelief. It's a kind of fable, and for me that's what made it rewarding. I don't think it's meant to be read realistically."

"He's a dentist," the famous writer said. "He's not an alchemist. Money is money. Why go chasing after gold?"

"I would love it if he were an alchemist."

"I kept expecting him to sell cocaine. Don't they have access to cocaine?"

"And laughing gas."

"But that's harder to sell."

"True."

"So I see him trying the thing with the gold teeth, and it's not working, and so he starts selling cocaine, and also he starts using cocaine, and that's when he spirals down."

"He doesn't spiral down. That's not the same story. I think we need to honor the writer's intentions."

"The writer needs to demonstrate that he knows about dentistry before we honor anything. It's his job to win us over."

"I *hate* going to the dentist."

"Everyone does."

"I was hoping he'd do more with that. Keep the reader in a state of anxiety."

"That's kind of a cliché, isn't it, being afraid of the dentist?"

"With good reason."

"What if we just took all the gold teeth out of the story? What are we left with then?"

"No motive."

"But that could be good. It would have a sense of ennui."

"I'm tired of ennui."

"It wouldn't be funny."

"It's not funny now."

"I thought it was funny."

"Nobody else did. Did anyone else think this was funny?"

"It could have been funnier."

And the conversation went on like this for another half hour before the famous writer stopped them to read from his notes aloud, as a way of summarizing their assessment of the story and wrapping up the discussion. Then he added, though he'd given no indication during the entire class that he'd felt this way, "I thought it was a fine story. You should send this one out."

§

The famous writer felt quite lonely on his walk over to his MG, which he'd learned to put the top up on, no matter what the weather, and he'd drive it that way, despite its being a nice night, because he'd also learned that driving the MG at night with the top down was a good way to get bugs in his teeth. And since he had every intention of bedding his girlfriend, it was not a good night for bugs in the teeth.

He started the car and sat with the engine idling as he texted her to let her know what had happened and his feelings about it. He was aesthetically opposed to sending long text messages, but she hadn't replied, so he sent three in a row, which he was also opposed to. There had been a rumor that he was dying. It got him thinking about his mortality, and about love, the deep kind of love they shared as well as the carpe diem kind of love they also shared. He waited to let that sink in before he sent the third text, a more direct invitation for a night together with no pressure sex-wise, though he was really hoping. Are you in the mood for Chinese?

Because he really did feel the possibility of his life ending too soon, and he couldn't just sit there, he was going to have to drive around, with the top up, which defeated the purpose of owning an MG, especially on a night like this. And after his third circuit around the university drive, where he was ogling the same young women walking, so that he was giving off a creepy vibe, he knew he was going to have to leave campus and go somewhere else, though not too far, since his girlfriend's apartment was nearby, and when she replied he wanted to be able to arrive in no time. He knew never to go there uninvited. He'd done that once and there was no way in hell he wanted to have to defend against what she was certain he didn't have the right to expect of her.

His phone was in the passenger seat and he stole glances at it as he drove, and also openly stared at the young women out walking, who were new to him tonight at least, now that he was on the far end of campus. As he came to the entrance to the university, he slowed, as he always did, because it was a tricky intersection where there tended to be a line of cars waiting to merge into traffic, but he didn't stop, because he didn't expect too many cars out at night, and there was a beautiful young woman who held hands with a boy who didn't deserve her, and the famous writer stared at her, and she noticed, but the boy didn't, and she smiled. He hoped she'd smiled because she recognized him and knew who he was, just as his phone lit up, the call he'd been waiting for from his girlfriend, and a massive black SUV moving much too quickly around the blind curve that led into this intersection met the driver's side of the famous writer's

MG, that did not have the right of way, and the small car tumbled and threw the famous writer through the soft vinyl roof and into the well-manicured grass at the edge of campus, and the beautiful young woman he'd been staring at and somehow managed to keep eye-contact with as he flipped and spun, screamed, and her male friend who didn't deserve her, looked up in horror to witness the famous writer's last moments as he met gravel, then grass, and his body opened to spill a streak of blood and came to rest in a pile of meat and broken bones. The famous writer experienced the accident in slow-motion and his eyes were open but not looking in any particular direction as he had a wide-open awareness of the whole scene, and his place in it, the beautiful young woman who ran over to him, above him now like a glowing angel, the boy she was with in shock and stopped in his tracks behind her, and she said his name, she *had* known him, though recognition of who she was eluded him. She was an angel, an angel who would escort him to eternity. And his phone was glowing in the grass, his girlfriend calling him back, his ringtone Vivaldi's Trio Sonata No. 12 "La Follia," and he heard the SUV driver, who had parked not far from the scene, his vehicle unscathed given the massive differential between his black beast and the fleet MG. He was beneath a baseball cap that kept his eyes in shadow under the street lights and he shouted again and again, "He came out of nowhere! He's at fault! I didn't see him!"

And the angel turned, she walked over to the phone that broadcast Vivaldi, which, in the dying writer's expanded awareness seemed as clear and rich sounding as when he'd seen it performed by the Atlanta Philharmonic, and the phone vibrated, and she hung up on the famous writer's girlfriend to dial 911 but the music continued. This was the unthinkable end for him. He wouldn't be able to say what he had wanted to tell his girlfriend at the Chinese restaurant. That he was bored with looking at the young women and he hadn't touched any of them anyway in years, and here they were together, at the same spot on the planet and in love, at least he was, and whatever they called it, whatever the expectations or legal obligation, he wanted to be with her in the mornings and the nights and to be able to arrive where she lived without permission and without being chased off. It seemed like a pittance now, with the curtain descending, but it was what he wanted more than anything, and the young woman, who didn't appear at all like an angel now, but like a girl, a cute girl, yes, but he had somehow gleaned an appearance of her that wasn't real. She was short, her thighs thick in her tight jeans, her hair frizzy with split ends. These were his last thoughts, confronted with the unidealized unattractive qualities of a girl he'd seen all wrong, and he hovered above his body and above the scene, looking down at his crumpled MG, a barely scratched black SUV, a boy and a girl, and a baseball-hatted protesting driver who'd recklessly removed him from life. He waited for the black unknown unknowable to erase him as he wallowed in his disappointment of the MG's inability to withstand a collision, of his girlfriend not calling sooner, of the beautiful angel being less than beautiful and not an angel, of the baseball-hatted boy for showing no compassion and no remorse, and of the ambulance for doing everything in their power to get there, but still arriving too late. His girlfriend would be irritated with him for not picking up, so she hadn't learned what had happened to him for several hours. And Lydia, his secretary, would be irritated that with no immediate family, it would fall on her to write his obituary and make his arrangements.

§

Last year, they'd hired a junior professor to teach the overflow workshops and the classes the famous writer didn't want to teach. The department chair, a white guy, from the literature side of the department, a Shakespeare scholar who, along with several other gray-haired white guys who were hired in the nineteen-seventies and -eighties, pretty much ran the English Department, the logistical end anyway—a Chaucer guy, a Wordsworth guy, an Eliot guy, a Washington Irving guy, and a poet who was technically a part of the Deep South Writers Workshop though he tended to pal around with the literature professors and he saw himself as more of a poetry scholar than a poet. They'd always let the famous writer bring in graduate students and do his own thing over in the creative writing wing of the English Department, but when it came to the new hire, the junior fiction professor, they weren't at all subtle about the fact that he should hire a woman. They themselves, in their most recent hires had brought in a Woolf scholar, a Dickinson scholar, and an African-Americanist, and it was strongly suggested that the new fiction writer should be a woman to counter the patriarchal masculinity of the famous writer.

He hired a twenty-eight-year-old straight white woman out of Michigan named Sparrow Walsh, who had four good short story publications, at *Granta*, *Glimmer Train*, *Gargoyle*, and *Guernica*, and with each of these publications she had attached the same bio that claimed she was working on a novel, which no one doubted, but it created the expectation that if Sparrow Walsh went up for tenure at Deep South, she would have had three years to write that thing, and to get it published, separate but equally daunting tasks. When the department chair saw the name Sparrow Walsh come across his desk to approve the hire, he warmed with anticipation that they might get their first Native American professor, but when Sparrow arrived she was as white as could be, her parents obviously hippies, and she was by no means organized or driven enough to run the Deep South Writers Workshop, which was precisely the position she was in when the famous writer was blotted out by a black SUV on the edge of campus.

Thankfully, Lydia was experienced at all the levers, and Deep South could continue for quite some time with Sparrow showing up early, sitting in the famous writer's office all day, and asking Lydia a lot of questions, because she had no idea how to do anything. Lydia resented that the twenty-eight-year-old made four times her salary, especially with the sudden expectation that she be subordinate to her, but Lydia always saw herself as better than these bookish fops who so often had no common sense, and the rewarding part of the job was that they had always needed her to hold it all together. When she walked into the famous writer's office she generally saw Sparrow standing in front of his bookshelves and taking mental inventory of the spines of the books. Or Sparrow would be at his desk reading one of them. All she needed to do in the junior fiction writer position was to write and to keep the famous writer happy by figuring out the university-related things he didn't want to do and to do them. Like all the junior fiction writers before her, just being here for a couple of years would help her get a better job, far from Mississippi, and it was what each successive Sparrow Walsh had done. Now she was expected to *be* him, and she wasn't up for that at all. Her response was to sit in his office, which, however long she occupied, would always be his office.

For her part, Lydia was glad not to have to put up with the whims of the famous writer but less than pleased that she had to babysit the new hire. She was confident in her ability to run the place and glad to be needed, though it created a lot more work for her, and more than a junior fiction writer they had always really needed a second secretary. The thing she was most glad of — though she would never admit this — was that her lie about the famous writer's being in his last days had turned out to be true. So when she got a call from Allison Avett, who was finalizing plans for the reunion, Lydia told her, because Allison hadn't heard, and Allison felt the fruits of all her hard work slipping away. There would be no reunion, she'd never get to meet Austin Goldman, and she wouldn't get the chance to workshop a better story than Maya Drake's.

Except that Lydia suddenly saw a way to turn their reunion into a memorial service, and it would save Lydia the trouble of having to make the plans, since Allison had already done most of the legwork for her reunion. She could ask the funeral director to keep the famous writer refrigerated for an additional three weeks, and they could all get together over spring break, just as they'd planned, when the literature professors, who never really liked the famous writer, would all be gone, and the people coming in from out of town would even have the option to rent dorm rooms. Allison followed Lydia's advice and she went back over her invitations and changed the wording from "reunion" to "memorial service," and from "kickoff party" to "wake." Her mentor was dead and she didn't know how to feel. She had supposedly accepted that he was passing, but she'd mostly been thinking of herself through all of this and his quick exit was unexpected. Because she didn't like not knowing what to feel, she got on Twitter and tweeted out the news about the famous writer's death, and she added a few nice things about what he had meant to her, and she tweeted some of the encouraging words he'd said to her over the years. News of his death hadn't gotten out beyond the local paper yet, and her phone lit up with each new fave her tweets received. She didn't know what to feel about his dying, but she felt good about having known him, and of being associated with him. She was by no means a Minimalist, but she respected the aesthetic and was proud to have studied the tenets of Minimalism: fewer words, more direct representation, less is more, or as he used to tell them, "For God's sake get over yourselves!" And she tweeted that out too.

After she got off the phone with Allison, Lydia realized she had to tell Sparrow about the reunion the former graduates had planned and how this was now going to be the famous writer's memorial service. It meant delaying getting him in the ground, which in Mississippi, until recent years, would have been unheard of, and it probably also violated some kind of cultural taboo, but Lydia was pretty much in charge now and this was the best way to please everyone and also get others to do the work.

Sparrow stood on the famous writer's office chair, which was on rollers and also reclined, so she had put herself in a precarious position, but she was trying to reach a book with an orange cover on the top shelf, his bookshelves nearly as high as the ceiling.

"You should be careful," Lydia said, the same as if she were talking to her four-year-old grandson reaching for a *Blue's Clues* DVD in a vertical stack sure to topple over on him.

"I've got it," Sparrow said, but the chair rolled away from the bookshelf and she held on, with very little control over what was about to happen.

With the same quick poise she would use on her grandson, Lydia pushed the rolling chair back toward the bookshelf, so that Sparrow could retrieve the orange book and climb down from the chair unharmed.

"Must be a good book."

"*Vida Urbana!* It's a favorite."

"We've got a lot of former students who want to come to his funeral. We're postponing the ceremony to accommodate them. I need you to sign off on this. We're going to loosen up some funds. We take from the journal, with no one expecting an issue any time soon. We take from the travel fund, since he's not going to any conferences or readings. We gain his salary back for the rest of the year. We pencil in a raise for me, to be approved by the dean and provost, and while you don't get a raise, per say, we can get you a one-time bonus, say $5,000, for your additional duties and the psychological damage of losing all your writing time. We come away with enough money for a very good party appropriate for the celebration of a man of his stature."

"Sounds fun," Sparrow said. She was already used to signing things without reading them. Lydia could have gotten away with anything in her current position, but she would content herself with the raise she'd given herself, her very low salary suddenly doubled and still a lot lower than Sparrow's.

"I haven't thought at all about writing," Sparrow said. In fact, she was pleased to have an excuse to not have to write. The novel she'd advertised in all of her bios in all of the literary journals where she'd published was a mess. She had chosen a historical period and region of Pennsylvania that was a lot harder to research than she'd expected when she'd decided to expand her *Granta* story, which worked as a short story, but as a novel there was all of a sudden all these *details* she had to somehow imagine or discover. Being in Mississippi made her want to write a novel set in Mississippi, except everything was still too new, she had to let Mississippi grow on her more. And she needed a plot. All she had was a character, a young woman in her late twenties who had moved for a job, a teaching job, but that was as far as she'd gotten, since not enough had happened to the thinly veiled version of herself. Until now. She suspected that in the new novel she hadn't written one word of yet, her character would have just gotten to the school when the principal was hit by a school bus and killed and for some reason she hadn't worked out yet, everyone expected her to become the replacement principal. She didn't know anything about being a principal, but like everyone else, she had gone to high school, so she figured faking the principal thing would be easier than faking historic Pennsylvania. As she sat at the famous writer's desk and tried to read *Vida Urbana!* she decided the school colors of the high school would be purple and yellow, and their mascot would be the mountain goats. There were no mountains anywhere in Mississippi, but she didn't care. They were going to be the Jackson County High School Mountain Goats and her character would demonstrate far more resourcefulness in running the place than she had, the high school secretary always calling in sick to stay home and watch soaps since the first change at JCHS was to get rid of the annoying TV that was always on in the main office. Sparrow would have started typing her new novel that afternoon, except she didn't know the famous writer's password and so she couldn't use his computer. Sooner or later, she'd get Lydia to put in an order for a new computer, but she decided she didn't want that to complicate the shifting around of the budget, so she would go for as long as she could as Interim Director without using one.

§

Because her phone kept lighting up with faves and retweets, Allison spent most of the day on Twitter, where she saw an article Maya had written, also getting a lot of attention. She pulled it up to see a three-page remembrance that Maya had very quickly puked onto the page and *Atlantic Online* had published. Allison had been wasting her time with tweets when she could have written an essay, like Maya had, and Maya beat her to it, and now there wasn't much point.

Allison was immediately put off by what she read. There was no mention of the famous writer setting Maya up with an agent, but it was as if what she had learned from him, to take left turns, was all that she had needed to earn her success. Allison couldn't remember the famous writer ever using the term "left turns" but she knew what Maya meant. He also didn't teach "left turns" as a method; he merely applauded what he saw in Maya's stories when she was able to pull it off, Maya's essay not bothering to mention all the times she'd put in a "left turn" only to have it ruin the story with everyone baffled by the choice. But in her best work, she brought back a minor character at the end and put them in a dialogue. Or an action forever changed the outlook of a character. Or a flashback would subvert reader expectation and hover there on a central conceit before returning to the characters where Maya had left them. Allison hated that Maya was really good at this, and how she had suddenly credited the famous writer for it, who had only been present in the workshops where she developed her signature technique, which had nothing to do with Minimalism, and which he was as opposed to as everyone else when it didn't work.

Maya painted the famous writer as wise and kind, able to see the kernel of art in order to bring it out. There was no mention of the time he had made Trent cry by mocking his best efforts, or of the many secretaries who stormed out of his office within a week of being hired in the long procession before Lydia. Allison knew that the eulogized often came off better than they were, and this was appropriate, but it still bothered her that the literati who hadn't known him, who thought of him as a minor player in the short-lived American Minimalist movement of the early nineteen-eighties would now think of him as larger than he was, which was exactly what Allison craved, though she didn't want to have to die to achieve it.

When her husband, Scott, got home, she continued to stew over the way the famous writer's death hadn't given her the advantages she sought. She supposed he was lucky to have died quickly, so close to the campus that was his home, as opposed to willowing away with whatever disease he'd succumb to, and she realized she didn't know. Maya hadn't mentioned it. Lydia hadn't said anything about it. Trent hadn't. Brain cancer sounded about right. Though maybe it was bone, blood, or pancreas. And she had no idea. She'd been so selfish through all of this she'd never even thought to ask. She Googled around on her laptop but there were no answers, her face frozen between anger and disgust, so that Scott broke with protocol while she was at her workspace and he asked, "What's-a-matter, Hon?"

"Maya Drake wrote a fucking essay."

"She wasn't supposed to?"

"*I* was going to. And now I can't. And none of what she wrote is true."

"Are we still going down there?"

"I told you we are. Yes. It's a funeral now instead of a reunion."

"What about workshopping? Is it still that?"

"I don't see how it could be," Allison said. She realized she was directing all of her frustration over Maya and the way the stupid *Atlantic* went along with her B.S. at Scott, as she often did, but he'd come to expect it, so he was unfazed.

"You should still workshop," he said. "It might be powerful. More so than having him there."

"You think?"

"Oh yeah," he said. "Because you're trying to please someone who ain't there. With each of you imagining some different version of him. It would be like taking all that baggage from over the years and dumping it there in Petal Mississippi."

"You think that would work? Like we'd finally be free of him or something?"

"And free of each other, to some extent."

Allison stopped Googling and she pulled up Facebook to send Trent an instant message. He was the one who had put forward the idea of the last workshop and she wanted to tell him what Scott had said, which was pretty convincing. Scott wasn't intellectual, or a reader, or someone who even really had a sophisticated understanding of symbolism, but every now and then he'd surprise Allison with something so perfectly right that she fell in love with him again.

Trent had posted his own remembrance, which Allison really liked since he was able to pay homage while also not going too far to create a fantasy version of the famous writer. While he didn't come out and admit that Colonel Kurtz had made him cry, he did hint at a darker side that wasn't always in service of making the story better or of developing thick skins in young writers. Trent had gotten a lot of likes, and a few shares, and Allison clicked the like button herself, which didn't seem enough, given the circumstances. She added her own comment to the long list of writers who were mutual Facebook friends who had mostly written some version of

"Sorry for your loss." Allison wrote, "This is beautiful, Trent. You really captured his spirit and what was best about him. I think he would have loved this."

Trent immediately liked her comment and since he was online she went ahead and sent him a private message: "I think we should still workshop. Are you in?"

"Who would lead it?"

"We don't need anyone to lead it. There were days he hardly said anything. It's more about us now anyway. When else will we ever get together? We need to go ahead and do this."

"You think people will send out stories in time to read them?"

"I do."

"It'll be fun," Trent said. "No, 'fun' isn't the right word. It'll be good, and special, and important."

"I think so too. Do you know what he was dying of?"

"He got hit by a truck."

"Before that. What was his disease?"

"I think it was a heart-something."

"They can fix that usually."

"I don't know," Trent said. "I didn't ask."

"Me neither. I bet Maya knows. She stayed in touch with him."

"*I* stayed in touch with him."

"They were closer."

"Do you think...?"

"No."

"I mean there was that student," Trent said.

"That was a long time ago," Allison said. "He learned his lesson. Anyway, I think Maya is asexual."

"She is not. I tried to kiss her once."

"That was me."

"Her too," Trent said. "Didn't go so well, but I got the impression she wouldn't be against it if I were just someone else."

"Isn't that always how it goes?"

"You got your dream guy."

"I wouldn't say that. He has been good for me, though."

"You going to ask Maya?"

"I might," Allison said. "There's this essay of hers. It's a good reason to contact her."

"You already had a reason."

"I know. I feel like she doesn't really like me sometimes."

"Maya doesn't hold grudges, I don't think."

"Why would she hold a grudge?" Allison said, "What did I do?"

"You were kind of jealous. You were pretty hard on her stories in workshop."

"Not any harder than anyone else."

"But also not really objective or fair."

"Reading isn't an objective experience."

"But if you had read the same story somewhere and it didn't have Maya's name on it, you'd probably like it."

"I guess."

"And you think she didn't know this?"

"Should I apologize or something?" Allison said. "That's acknowledging it. Shouldn't I play it cool?"

"You'll see her in a couple of weeks. You two can work it out then."

§

Since there wasn't much for Sparrow to do as the Interim Director of the Deep South Writers Workshop — Lydia pretty much had it covered — she paced the famous writer's office and thought about the future, specifically about new courses she might teach in the fall. It occurred to her that as the Interim Director she wouldn't need permission for any new classes, she could simply ask Lydia to put them on the schedule. This was the most freedom she'd ever felt when pondering the makeup of a syllabus, but also the most responsibility. There were rows of books by Minimalists, and she thought about the possibility of creating a class that was an homage to her deceased colleague. She remembered a great story he had told at a faculty party, when a group of Minimalists were drinking together at a conference, and Annie Lind challenged everyone to come up with a one-word story. They each chipped in twenty bucks, and the winner would come away with the pot, a fee that Carlson McDevors objected to but that everyone else agreed was pretty much the standard entry to any writing contest. Carlson ran his own contest at his press that had a twenty-five-dollar entry fee, though he explained that the winner of his contest got the manuscript published and the entry fees defrayed publication costs. The winner of the one-word-story contest, Annie Lind explained, would get to keep the cash pot and would have the great distinction of being recognized as the most minimal of Minimalists.

Annie's entry was "The," which was obvious and only clever if the reader let it roll around in the mind, which was inevitable, and so it was a pretty good story after all.

Carlson's was "Hollywood," which worked in its own way, but depended a lot on the nostalgia and myth that already surrounded the word. While Annie had gone with the least charged of words,

Carlson had chosen one with gold polish, which was fair. And why not? He said he was going to enter "pornography," but settled on "Hollywood" instead.

"Same thing," Arthur Doughtry snipped.

"No one says 'pornography'," Brett Braff said. "You have to say 'porn'."

Arthur Doughtry's word was, "Slift," which wasn't a word but did suggest a feeling and had the reader second-guessing if maybe it was a word after all. He didn't win, but it was a very good entry.

Brett Braff's was "Crisis," which was cheating a little, since he was basically saying "conflict," though "crisis" was more exaggerated and a word that tickled the ear.

The famous writer won the pot with his word, "Timpani." It may not have gone that way on another day with another group of Minimalists, but they loved his word, what it was and what it stood for. While "crisis" was abstract, "timpani" was concrete and one could hardly think of it without hearing it, booming or rolling to crescendo. "Crescendo" would have been a pretty good one-word-story too, but "timpani" was better. So good that Carlson McDevors offered to publish it as a broadside. He wanted the famous writer to give him the pot to defray the cost of publishing the broadside, and while the famous writer pondered it, he decided to keep the money and buy everyone drinks instead.

Sparrow Walsh loved the idea of teaching a class where she could tell such stories, and she only wished she had been to more faculty parties so she had more of the famous writer's anecdotes to tell. She took a sheet of paper from the printer and made a quick reading list of Minimalists as a draft of her syllabus. She listed everyone who was at the one-word contest party, of course, and a few more who were obvious. She decided she needed some diversity and wracked her brain for Minimalists of color and could only come up with Dre Andre. There had to be more. Her knowledge was lacking and after some more research she could surely come up with some non-white Minimalists. If she could use the computer she would look up Dre Andre to see who he was associated with, but she suspected it would be the writers she'd already named. She understood that writers didn't necessarily have to be lumped together by color or gender, and maybe there was more to be said about grouping them together as movements: the Minimalists, the Maximalists, the Middling-ists, the Post-Middling-ists, the Pre-Post-Middling-ists, the Junkie Crew, the Fictionauts, the Fictionistas, and of course, Anti-Poet. If it weren't already a thing, Sparrow thought "anti-poet" could have been her own one-word entry. If she were at that get together and if she were a Minimalist. She wanted to be. She would have liked to have been one, but she also liked words too much. She could fill a page quickly and maybe that was a talent and maybe it was a curse. With the right editor she could probably still be a Minimalist, though that time had mostly come and gone. She'd have better luck trying to join Anti-Poet.

Sparrow decided that maybe her class should be non-white writers, since she recognized it as a shortcoming of the Minimalists and of a few of the other movements too, even Junkie Crew, if it could be believed. The category 'Minimalist' was maybe too broad for a literature course, and so she decided that maybe non-white experimental writers would get her there. Obviously "experimental" was a problematic term that was going to defy definition, but she'd get the class talking about it the first few sessions and they would come away with ideas about who was and who was not considered experimental. The famous writer, for example, was not considered experimental, though Minimalism was a kind of experiment. She suspected that only when it was taken to the extremes of say, a one-word story, could Minimalism qualify as truly experimental. She suspected the famous writer would have been okay with that, since having been mainstream certainly helped him live the writer's life. He would have found all writing, at least all writing that was worth anything, to have been experimental. The writer set out not knowing where the writing would lead, after all. And sometimes the writer succeeded and sometimes the writer failed. That, to him, was the very definition of an experiment, and to try to draw other distinctions wasn't helpful. There were writers who pushed at the edges more, who didn't care much about audience, who would rather challenge a reader than please a reader, and Sparrow suspected this was who we meant when we applied a label like "experimental," which, like it or not, was widely in use and did have meaning, even if it maybe wasn't the most objective or descriptive of terms.

Sparrow scribbled out a quick list of non-white experimental writers and she liked it so much she wanted to have the list typed out, and while she didn't have access to the famous writer's computer, she did have a secretary and so she burst from her office and she was about to ask Lydia to turn her grocery list of non-white writers into an MS Word file, but Lydia was on the phone, and her expression showed that the conversation was important. Lydia held up a finger to make it clear she did not want to be interrupted. Sparrow paced in front of Lydia's desk until she realized she was being rude and that what she wanted wasn't so important that it couldn't wait, and so she sat in one of the chairs outside the famous writer's office, where a student might, hypothetically, wait to see her. From Lydia's perspective, Sparrow—in a sundress, sandals, and the spangly jewelry she always wore—could most certainly have been mistaken for a student waiting outside the famous writer's office.

Lydia had called the famous writer's girlfriend, who she had spoken to a couple of times since he'd died, but Lydia realized she had taken over too much of the planning for his memorial and she wanted to be sure the girlfriend didn't have ideas of her own.

Lydia explained, "Some of the graduates of the program were planning a reunion when this happened. We were thinking of putting off the ceremony until closer to when they had planned to come down, and that way more of them could participate. If it's okay with you, that is.

"Splendid," Lydia said. "Yes, they can keep the body.

"I don't know," Lydia said. "I can ask. I would suggest maybe his agent.

"Someone *besides* his agent?" Lydia said. "I mean that's what an agent does.

"I understand. Can do. I'll send you the details so far and the mailing list of the former students who have said they are coming. Is there anything else? Please don't hesitate to ask."

And as soon as she hung up, Lydia explained to Sparrow, "That was his girlfriend. He had a novel on his computer and she wants someone to look at it."

"I could take a look," Sparrow said. "I mean I'm kind of busy with the directorship and all, but I'd find time."

"She said not you."

"Specifically?"

"Yes."

"Why?"

"Not a fan of your work, I guess."

"Oh."

"She's just a girlfriend," Lydia said. "She's no expert. Don't take it personally."

"Who does she want?"

"She wants to look at writing samples from former students and she'll select someone."

"A contest?"

"I guess."

"And what do they win?"

"They get to read the manuscript and talk about it with her."

"That's it?"

"I mean she wants to sell it, obviously. There was a will and she's the executor of his estate. She gets his royalties. She wants to know if it's any good. And not just if it's good, but if it's good-good or great-good."

"Great-good would be great."

"That's what she thinks. She just wants someone else to tell her. Someone she can trust."

"And she'll know whether or not to trust them by looking at their writing?"

"This is what she believes, yes."

§

When the famous writer's girlfriend's email went out to everyone Allison Avett was as charged as if she'd gotten a thousand retweets. She could win this contest with the famous writer's girlfriend and go into the workshop with everyone knowing she'd won, and then she could win the workshop too. More importantly, if she had the famous writer's last manuscript, Austin Goldman would have to talk to her. She'd have him right where she wanted him. She fantasized that she could send him her own novel manuscript and tell him it was the famous writer's, just to see him make glowing remarks about her work, and only then would she tell him she'd made the switcheroo. Of course, she didn't have a novel manuscript. And what was it, then, she hoped to gain from the famous writer's literary agent? She wanted him to be her agent too, obviously, she just didn't have a novel at the moment. She would have one, eventually. Maybe next year or the year after that. And she remembered she had short stories, enough to compile a collection. Her own agent had told her no way could she sell her stories, but her own agent wasn't Austin Goldman. She'd win the girlfriend's contest, she'd get her hands on the famous writer's last manuscript, she'd tease Austin Goldman with how great it was, meanwhile working on a novel of her own, the best one she'd ever written, and she'd also get him to look at a collection of her stories. It was a pretty good plan, and she was truly sorry that the famous writer had died and that his girlfriend was left to clean up after him, but she was far more motivated than before, when the idea of the famous writer leading them in a last workshop had her thinking she could blow them all away. Now she could blow them away, but the stakes seemed higher.

Allison saw that Trent Sanivaugh was online and she sent him an instant message.

"Did you get the email from Kurtz's girlfriend?"

"Pretty crazy, right?"

"Are you going to send her something?"

"Why not?"

"What should I send?"

"Do you have anything new?"

She didn't. Trent was being evasive. He had liked her stuff well enough when they were in the writing program together, around the time of the awkward date, when, even though she made absolutely clear that she was not, he'd thought of her as a potential sexual partner. He was smart enough not to say it, but she knew her books weren't exactly his cup of tea. Precisely because of phrasing like that. She'd write something like "cup of tea," and then leave it in because she didn't know how else to say it. People still said "cup of tea," even if they hardly ever drank cups of tea anymore, so that one was unlikely to have a personal taste in teas, or to have a "*my* cup of tea.*" She had decided long ago that it was okay that she wrote like this, that she would reach more readers that way, and she had. Though for this next book, if she was going to be able to show it to Austin Goldman, she would have to cut that shit out.

"What of mine would you send her," Allison typed, "among what you've read?"

"The cocktail party scene."

She started to type, "Which cocktail party..." when she realized he was probably fucking with her. There were a lot of cocktail party scenes, none standing out among others. She backspaced and typed, "Of my short stories. Do you have a favorite?"

This gave him permission to reach back to when they were young, and even if her own agent hadn't been optimistic about her stories, the work had a kind of energy that was lost in her novels that were overwrought and with the personality polished away.

"'The Depressed Girl'."

Of course he would like that one. It was the least like any of her others. It lacked a plot, it didn't have more than three characters, and there wasn't even a setting. It did a very good job of conveying how she felt that year, but she didn't feel that way anymore, hadn't for years and years, especially with Scott around. She understood why Trent had picked that one, but she couldn't send it to the famous writer's girlfriend. She couldn't really see it winning and so maybe she was going to have to write something new.

"What will you send?" she typed.

The first two sentences of the new story he had started popped into his head, "Joan followed the path into the woods. She had been there yesterday, with a boy who knew the trails, and she hoped to retrieve her lost locket." He had no idea where it was going or if he'd finish it in time.

"I can't decide," he replied. "I think I'll draw a title out of a hat."

"There you go. Don't send 'Duplicitous Miscreants'."

"It was meant to be ironic."

"That's no excuse."

"Okay. That one won't go in the hat."

"Do you think Maya will send one?"

"Of course."

"I don't care if I don't win," Allison typed, "so long as she doesn't win."

"You do too care if you don't win."

"So do you."

"But not as much as you. I know why Maya wins and I'm okay with that."

"The whole 'left turn' thingy?"

"That's part of why. It's a style."

"Random twists is a style?"

"They might be random at first," Trent replied, "but they make sense over time."

"I should write a Maya parody."

"You should write you. Dig down."

"Says the author of *Three Drummers, a Clarinet, and a Pennywhistle?*"

"Touché. I'll dig down too. Deal?"

§

When iMOL got the email from Bobby Knight's girlfriend that explained the contest and why she was doing it, he sent a Google Hangouts invite to Trisha A, to see what she thought of it all.

Her immediate response was, "I blogged this two days ago. Where have you been?"

"You blogged about his girlfriend? She asked us not to."

"Who said anything about his girlfriend? I blogged about his dying and used him as a metaphor for the patriarchy. It's finally happening. Women have taken over publishing and whether or not we get to run the show, we will at least have our voices heard."

"I think it's been that way since at least 1990."

"Has not."

"Edith Wharton won the Pulitzer Prize in 1921."

"She was rich. Doesn't count."

"Willa Cather, 1923. Anyway, *you're* rich."

"I renounced my elite stature. I blogged that like six years ago, remember?"

"You still spend the money."

"I'm a counter-force. People should be glad I have money."

"So the reunion is still on," iMOL said, "except now it's a funeral. His girlfriend sent an email. She has his last unpublished novel and she's going to let one of us read it, or edit it, or something. She wants a writing sample."

"Why didn't I get an email? I get Lydia's emails. I'm pretty much out there. I'm easy to contact."

"You may have been left off intentionally."

"That is so sexist."

"His girlfriend is a woman. I'll forward it to you."

"I'm sending a sample anyway. And a proposal. I could add marginalia to deconstruct the text as hegemonic and imperialistic. Instead of going with a publisher we could send the novel out via Twitter over a period of like thirty-six hours."

"I think she wants to sell it. I think she wants people to actually read it."

"I hate reading."

"Me too."

"A Kickstarter idea I had was to turn all novels into movies."

"Someone already had that idea. It's called Hollywood."

"Not Hollywood movies. Just movies."

"What will you send her?" iMOL said.

"A link to the blog."

"No."

"What then?"

"Write something."

"Like a story?"

"That's what's implied."

"Have you been writing stories?" Trisha A. said.

"Kind of. I use a Tarot deck. It's maybe not the best method but it works for me. I get the Fool a lot. And Death reversed. So far there have been a lot of stories about a nearsighted guy who almost dies."

"You're writing Mr. Magoo."

"I need a better deck. I'm thinking of trying I Ching."

"I don't think I learned one thing while I was at Deep South."

"Sure you did," iMOL said. "You just don't use it."

"You don't either."

"I could maybe write screenplays."

"I hear they're impossible to sell."

"So are novels. I could self-publish."

"A self-published screenplay?"

"Why not?"

Once the university chancellor and provost heard of the famous writer's death they also learned of Sparrow Walsh's promotion to Interim Director of the Deep South Writers Workshop. This put pressure on them to find his replacement but also shifted focus. There was a woman in charge, after all. It gave them one year to find another famous writer, probably not a woman, they realized, but also, probably not a white guy.

Lydia patched a phone call through to Sparrow in the famous writer's office. "It's the provost," she said, and Sparrow picked up.

"I need you to send us a job description," he said. "All the qualifications and duties of the former director. We've got to get a job ad out."

Sparrow had no idea what the famous writer did. It seemed like Lydia was doing everything. She started by making a list of all the things Lydia did. And then she remembered some of the things the famous writer did on his own.

Teach upper-level fiction workshops. Read applications of prospective graduate students. Write recommendation letters. Edit

The Deep South Triannual. Mentor writers. Invite and schedule visiting writers for the Ingram Trust Visiting Writer's Series.

Shit.

Sparrow realized there were writers, editors, and agents scheduled to visit as part of this series. She didn't know if they were still obligated to come, or if they would still want to come, since they mostly came to hang out with the famous writer. Could the money be reallocated to his funeral fund? Could she invite some writers of her own, maybe one or two non-white experimental writers as a warm-up for the class she was planning? She pulled up the list of visiting writers from the email Lydia had sent out six weeks ago and saw the next writer was scheduled the week before the famous writer's memorial, and she wasn't a writer but a literary agent, a good one, Holly Rorsch. Sparrow knew that she was just the kind of writer Holly Rorsch might represent, and so she decided not to cancel. On the contrary, she had reason to contact her, to make sure she would still come, because meeting Holly, especially under these kinds of memorable circumstances, could lead to good things for Sparrow down the road.

"Lydia," she shouted without getting up from the famous writer's desk. "Can you get me Holly Rorsch on the line?"

"I have her phone number," Lydia shouted back. "Do you want me to write it down."

"Please," Sparrow said, "and bring it to me." But then she thought better. She wasn't really comfortable telling Lydia what to do, and Lydia certainly wasn't comfortable with it either. "I'll come get it. Thanks."

She didn't expect Holly Rorsch to actually answer her phone. Most literary agents were very clear that writers should never ever call them, and that if there was anything that needed discussion they would be the ones to call. But Holly picked up immediately.

"Hi," Sparrow said, "I'm calling from the Deep South Writers Workshop."

"I saw it on my caller ID," Holly said. "I was expecting you to be the dead guy."

"So you heard?"

"It's been on social media."

"We still want you to come," Sparrow said. "If we brought you in a week later than originally scheduled a lot of his former students will be here, and you'd be part of his memorial. It doesn't have to be anything formal. It doesn't have to be about Minimalism. You could simply be here and do your thing, whatever that might be, and we'd be pleased to have you."

"I wasn't sure what was going to happen, so I didn't make other plans. I'd be happy to make an appearance."

"There'll be readings and his girlfriend has organized some kind of a contest."

"Why?"

"He had an unpublished novel. She wants one of them to look at it."

"That's what I do," Holly said and she perked up at her unbelievable luck. "I'd be happy to take a look."

"I'm not saying she'd be against it," Sparrow said, "but she wants one of them to see it first."

"Whatever for?"

"It's her book now," Sparrow said. "She can do what she wants with it. She didn't want me to look at it either. We're all going to have to play along."

"I see. What about Goldman?"

"I don't know if she told him. But he will be here too. He'll learn of it soon enough."

"I'm most definitely coming. You can count on it."

§

The famous writer's girlfriend hadn't quit her job but she'd quit showing up and there was no expectation that she ever would. She could sell the famous writer's house or live in it. She could sell his last novel. She could spend his money. These days she stayed in her pajamas in her apartment as she ate cereal all day. She sat on the couch facing the TV that was off and she read from her laptop. Four stories had come in already and she remembered the nights early on in their relationship when he would complain about the reading he had to do, when she wanted to watch a movie, or drink with him, and he had his student's stories he had to read. She had also been one of the writing students but quit going when he reciprocated her interest. She didn't want to be accused of anything. Workshops could be nasty enough.

He did his writing in his office at the university, mostly in the mornings, so once they were a thing it never seemed to get in the way, but there were all these budding young artists who took so much of his time. He didn't read their stuff as much once he and the girlfriend settled into a routine, and they did watch movies or drink or whatever, but she hadn't given up on being a writer yet and wanted to know if she'd saw in their work what he'd seen, because he would sometimes talk with her about their stories, and though she'd never read them, she was dogmatic about plotting and believability, and she was pretty sure he sometimes took her feedback to the workshop. She wanted to know the difference between an amateur writer and a writer like the famous writer, and she was mostly afraid she wasn't going to be able to tell. She liked his books well-enough but he wasn't perfect and on any given day if she had a choice between one of his novels and a Will Ferrell movie, there wasn't going to be too much hand-wringing over which she would choose. He knew this about her, of course, and he knew it was also true of the majority of English speakers. He understood the joy of a Will Ferrell movie and wished he were making those instead of books half the time anyway. So his audience was a narrow one who engaged in the antiquated activity of novel reading because they thought it made them better, and they eschewed Will Ferrell movies at the same time they overestimated the pleasures of a good novel, because they read bad novels too, with equal aplomb, and so she had no idea who to trust when it came to assessing the value of the writer and their writing. She most especially did not trust the famous writer's colleagues on the literature side of the English Department, because although they made a living at praising books and of teaching students how to assess literature, they almost never read living writers or showed up for any of the Deep South readings or events, which were sometimes boring, but she put on a dress and she went, and she was often enough pleasantly surprised by what went on, which had been easy to forget in her time away from the program.

She suspected the literature professors were motivated by a desire to control the past and to claim ownership over it, and the famous writer agreed with her, though he mostly boiled down his commentary about his English Department colleagues, including the poet, to, "They're a bunch of grown-up teacher's pets. They're pompous pricks. They would probably *hate* Shakespeare if they ever met him, and vice versa. They lack the spark of imagination and they value the intellect above all else, which is another way of saying they value themselves above all else. They seem to almost believe that they've *made* the dead writers they adore and they see *analysis* of a book as replacing the book."

There was no way in hell the famous writer's girlfriend was going to let any of the professors look at his last book, and while the stories sent to her so far were mostly flawed, she knew that his students had different ideas about literature, as living, as playful and representative of the best in us, and she was reassured that her idea of seeking out one of his writers was the best way for her to move forward with his manuscript, which she hadn't read very much of, because it was painful, and she wanted one of them to do that work, and to talk with her about it, the same way the famous writer talked about their work with her, where she didn't have to read it but she could still say what might make a character's actions more believable or what might make for a better ending. The famous writer had a skill that could only be put in service with the help of an edifice like the Deep South Writers Workshop. She had a talent that only the famous writer had recognized and had known how to make use of. Given that he wasn't even reading the stories there toward the end, she could have taken over his job better than Sparrow Walsh, though the idea of her doing that would be preposterous to anyone with the power to hire her. Right now there was someone in the Chancellor's office combing the Internet for an emerging writer of color who was under the radar enough that they didn't already teach at a writing program in a fantastic city. Not to say this imagined writer did or didn't possess the same level of story-fixer talent that the famous writer's girlfriend had, but the drive toward diversity was going to override everything, even if the students were all white, even if the writer of color they would hire would also leave in two years for somewhere better, as expected, as was right, and the writer's girlfriend would stay here in Petal, unaffiliated with the program, except for that one time she'd convinced them all to send her their best stuff.

§

As Lydia left campus she circled back around because of the construction of the new polymer sciences building and she took an exit she rarely did, because of the blind curve and the students who drove too fast on that road, and she saw there was an impromptu memorial at the spot where the famous writer had been killed. There were bundles of flowers, a few of his paperbacks, and a Styrofoam cross with his first and middle name on the horizontal, and his last name down the vertical. He was an atheist, of course, but the gesture didn't seem inappropriate or disrespectful, it only showed there were a lot of students who didn't know very much about him. Lydia pulled over to let the other cars around her and she walked over and took one of the paperbacks. It was relatively new, thought the spine had been broken, so it had been read. Lydia had started reading that one when she first took the job here, and she had liked it, until she got to know the famous writer and his flaws, mostly his mean-spirited joking around, and she lost all desire to continue reading, even though she was quite sure the novel was good and she'd been enjoying it. She felt better about him now, and she decided she'd go ahead and finish his book, his most popular one. He'd given her the job, he hadn't fired her though he'd shown a propensity to, and she figured she owed him at least that.

As soon as she started driving again and she had pulled out into traffic, Lydia's phone rang and she saw the call was from the dead writer. It gave her a chill but she redoubled her efforts to pay attention and she drove another block before she answered.

It was Sparrow, of course. She said Austin Goldman was calling her asking about a manuscript and she didn't know what to say.

"Tell him you don't have it," Lydia said.

"He'll ask me who does, and I don't think he should be bothering his girlfriend, at least not now. He should let her alone."

"He's going to do what he's going to do. Would mean the rest of us seeing it a lot sooner, probably."

"I suppose. I've invited another literary agent to his memorial. Maybe I'll tell him this other agent has it."

"That could be fun. Invite a bunch of them."

"Maybe I will."

"This can wait," Lydia said. "I'm on my way home."

"Right," Sparrow agreed. "Sorry to bug you."

"It could have waited."

"I guess I worry too much. I'm afraid I'll do something wrong."

"I won't let you. Think of it like this: he used to sit in there and write. He'd make students wait forty minutes minimum before he'd see them. His girlfriend would visit and they would lock the door. There is nothing you can do that is going to have any effect on this program one way or another. Students are going to come. New writers like you will be hired to teach and they will also come and go."

"You're the only constant," Sparrow said. "You totally deserved that raise. He should have done it a long time ago."

"Thank you, Sparrow. There were probably fifty candidates for your job that I'd have chosen over you, but you're not so bad. Maybe on some level he knew what he was doing."

§

Once, when the famous writer's laptop was stolen at a coffee shop, his girlfriend went into a panic while he remained calm. He could get a new laptop. He could even buy one that same day. And he had an elaborate system of backups. He divulged his most common passwords to his girlfriend and while she had the urge to write them down he repeated them back to her in a way that made them easy to remember. She could try variations on three or four of his passwords and she should have access to all of it, including the will, which she refused to look at, but that was saved in a file called "will" in a folder of the same name. He had told her enough about the will over the years. The agent would handle anything related to his books, for his fifteen percent, and all she had to do was collect checks. He had various files of unfinished manuscripts and the one book, which he'd finished years ago, but he was saving. His critical acclaim was on a slow decline, like a helium balloon that deflated over days, but he still sold books, and he held on to his best novel for the right time, which happened to be now, since he was dead.

The girlfriend had had a chance to spend time with the body in the hospital morgue, but that was weeks ago. They had stitched the open places together, with little regard for cosmetic appearance, since that was the mortician's job, and the famous writer had achieved closed-casket status. She didn't think of the body as him, because he was inanimate, colorless, and cold, and she wondered if he were more whole, if he looked more like himself, would she feel the same way?

It didn't bother her that a few real estate agents contacted her to see what she might do with his house. They'd gotten her name from the obituary and from there she was easy to find. They were polite and genuinely seemed to want to help. She told them she wasn't selling just yet, but she would. Students were coming down, and although dorm rooms had been made available, his house was the right place to host a party where some of them could also sleep over if they needed to. His house had a wrap-around porch with a row of white rocking chairs and ceiling fans, the place about as Southern as could be, though they never used those rockers. It was always too hot, or the mosquitos would feast on anyone who dared spend time outdoors. She imagined the students would be the first to finally rock in them, with cigarettes, and reminiscing.

Her apartment had a balcony she almost never used for the same reason. She had a couple foldable aluminum lawn chairs out there and a potted fern. She used to smoke on this balcony and tamp out the butts in the soil of the fern, but she'd given it up. She was one of the lucky ones who could quit. She missed smoking sometimes, but surprisingly didn't miss it at the moment. She sat at her kitchen table, with coffee, and she went through the emails on her phone, to read the stories his students had sent her. She was leaning toward Maya Drake, who had sent a story about a couple in an apartment building who called the police for a noise complaint about another couple in the same building, and the arrival of the police set off a series of events that led to this other couple losing custody to child protective services and the first couple trying anything and every-thing to avoid the guilt of their role in the boy being taken away, until eventually they were friendly enough that the first couple was asking the second couple to get them drugs, and the two couples smoked drugs and listened to loud music together, something that never would have happened if the second couple still had their kid.

But the famous writer's girlfriend looked up Maya and the first thing that came up in the search was the piece she'd written about the famous writer's death. It was well-written but it bothered the girlfriend. She wanted someone who wouldn't go public with her feelings, as Maya had, which she had every right to do, but for the girlfriend it meant Maya wasn't the right person for his last book. She'd also eliminated Allison. The girlfriend was going to give Allison's story a chance, but she only got as far as her title, "The Girl on the Bus," which seemed so much like all the titles these days that she went to the next email without reading any further. There was a marked difference in the stories from students who attended his workshops in more recent years. The work was shorter, often a lot shorter, and there was a tendency toward magic. In a story where a husband cheats on his wife, the wife puts a spell on him and they both suffer, he from the spell, she from descending into the black arts. In a story about the end of the world, it rains and rains, and everyone sinks, the last of us standing on tiptoes on rooftops as the oceans continued to rise. The story from Trent Sanivaugh was like neither of these groups and she returned to it. She liked his story but wasn't sure why. She supposed it was science fiction, which the famous writer despised, but she wasn't sure he would find anything here to make fun of. He hated any incarnation of tentacled humanoids, of cannibalistic rituals, of telekinesis or telepathy, or warp speeds and laser guns. Trent's story was in the near future, where psycho-analysis was left to computers, and his main character, who was having UFO abduction episodes, went seeking a human counselor who would believe her. She found one. He was basically someone who would listen, and as the story progressed, as this character recounted her abductions under hypnosis, the famous writer's girlfriend couldn't help but wonder if all the UFO stuff wasn't just cover to allow Trent to write a story about survivor's trauma, because his character was powerless against these alien visitors when they came, and the famous writer's girlfriend was unsettled and afraid when she read the story, even when she'd already read it and knew exactly where it was headed.

Trent didn't have a blog where he wrote about being a writer. He didn't have a book, and while he had published a few of his stories, his accolades—at least what she could find—didn't match his talent, at least as demonstrated by the story he'd sent. She was leaning toward Trent and she had to pick someone soon, so they'd have time to look over the famous writer's last book before everyone came down for his funeral. Whoever she selected might even choose an excerpt to read at the service.

She would make it a point to get out of the apartment, to pick up groceries, and to go to the university rec. center to do laps in the pool. She'd think about the students and the stories they'd sent. And if she didn't change her mind by tomorrow, she'd send Trent the famous writer's last book. She'd ask him to come on board as editor, or publicist, or whatever role he thought would best serve the book. She wanted him to read it and tell her what it was about. She wanted him to be honest and to tell her what was good and what could be better, and if what could be better was something he could make better, then he should do it. He'd be paid. He'd be credited in the acknowledgements. And all publisher inquiries would be directed to him. He could still have Austin Goldman agent the book, if he chose, or he could go with someone else. She would let it be up to him how and in what form this book would go out into the world. She suspected it would be soon, and it would be good, and she would read it then, after the world had re-affirmed the famous writer's genius. And it would be her way of saying goodbye to him, engaging with his work again for their last conversation. It was his last gift.

She needed to clear her head and to research this Trent Sanivaugh guy one more time. She didn't remember the famous writer ever talking about him, but here he was in her emails, and his work was good.

§

Trent was up late. Everyone else in the impromptu reunion workshop group had emailed their stories and he was supposed to have his out by midnight. Everyone would need a few days to read them all, and really even that was pushing it, because they weren't graduate students anymore. They had lives, with jobs and responsibilities. Trent was at his girlfriend's place. He was balancing spending time with her before he left and finishing his story. It wasn't the story that he sent to the famous writer's girlfriend. He felt he should send something else to the workshop. And he had gotten a new idea a few days ago that he was feverishly trying to shape into something coherent.

Trent's girlfriend was sprawled across the bed, wrapped in the sheets face-down and sleeping heavily. She had a small desk and chair, where mostly dirty laundry was piled to keep it off the floor, where Trent had put the dirty laundry anyway so he had a place to sit. The desk was toward the wall, where she had a framed poster of the Eiffel Tower lit up at night, interesting enough to stare into, but he didn't want his back to his girlfriend, so he moved the chair to the side of the desk, which had him hunched over, but he could watch her sleep and also look out the window at the silver maple whose leaves, lit by streetlight, waved in the breeze. He hadn't packed. He hadn't checked in with the airline through their website. He hadn't sent off the rent check. Everything was on hold. He would work until he felt dazed then he'd get jacked on coffee and work some more. He loved what he'd come up with but the ending was eluding him. It had to be surprising but also feel right for the story.

He had a general rule that no one ever died in his stories because it was hard to pull off. Removing a character felt like a play for sympathy, getting the emotions all ramped up because of an easy gesture. Someone was always going to be dissatisfied with that. He especially never killed off a character at the end of a story, which felt like cheating. But this time he might. He entertained the idea of a character dying, then he pushed it away. He thought of other possible endings, then rounded his way back to the death of the character. And the obvious question for him became, did he have to write a funeral? He hoped not. He didn't think so, but maybe?

He had looked at the files of the stories everyone else had emailed but didn't look at the stories. He couldn't. He did scan the titles, though. Maya's came in first, of course. And one of the younger writers, someone who went by iMOL had sent something called "Internet Log 4419." Trent was intrigued but also kind of put off by that. It was almost like sending a story called "story," but he would reserve judgment until he'd read it, and then maybe he'd give some advice about a new title, though he suspected that someone who went by iMOL wasn't going to listen to anyone about anything. He hoped "Internet Log 4419" would be good. He hoped he'd be pleasantly surprised and that iMOL would be generous and kind in his reading of the other writers' stories, but for now he had to resist the urge to read it and he had to continue with his own writing.

Midnight was an arbitrary deadline. No one was going to give him grief if it came in at dawn. But he did need to get it done, and he hoped the right idea that would give him a tidy ending would hit him soon.

2

Allison and Scott had four hours to kill in the Detroit Airport, which meant getting a bite to eat and some drinks. They would browse the stupid newsstand shops that carried more candy than books, with only the commercial titles, in paperback, and a few literary novels tossed in like chocolate chips. One of her proudest moments was when she and Scott spent part of her advance from her second novel on a long weekend at a resort in Cozumel, and they spotted her first book in an airport bookstore. She asked the cashier if maybe the store would like for her to sign them, but the woman didn't understand. She seemed to think that might be vandalism, and she explained to Allison that she could get in trouble if she said 'yes.'

"Congratulations on your book," she had said, "but I am not authorized to let you do that."

In the brief period before that uneasy rejection from the airport newsstand cashier Allison had gone from feeling like she'd made it to feeling like her credit card had been declined.

Scott travelled a lot, so she mostly let Scott decide where they would eat, where they would sit, and however else they might loiter to kill time. Allison was on high alert. She knew that all the other writers were also traveling across the country on their way to Mississippi, and as far from Mississippi as Detroit was, it was where they were sent to change planes, and she suspected a lot of other people on their way to the reunion might be in this same airport. Since it had been her idea, even though the gathering was technically a memorial service, it still felt like a reunion to her, and so she called it that, to herself, and to Scott, who wore a suit, even though he wasn't working, because he said Armani commanded respect and the trip would go more smoothly. They were flying on his Sky Miles, and he charged expenses to his business account. He would pay it all back, of course, but this was his natural habitat, and he was demonstrating for Allison how he made his living, because tax law was abstract and it mostly existed in law libraries and online databases, though it required meeting with representatives of large corporations housed in very tall buildings, in metropoli around the country. In fact, it was the traveling around part of the job that was even more important than the loopholes and shadow accounts he'd become expert at setting up, because he had to convince these other Armani men what he knew, which took charm. Anyone could learn a tax avoidance scheme. It was the impression one gave off as a legitimate accounts' redistributor and above-board swindler that got clients, and it was the whiff of success that kept them coming back. He dressed the part, he flew to where the money was made, he brought computer files home, he put the tax avoidance schemes in motion, he flew back to the Armani men with the good news, and the Armani men easily recognized him as one of their own.

As she tagged along, Allison almost forgot this was her trip, and that she was the one who had come up with the idea. She imagined she might run into Maya Drake as Transportation Security waved metal-detecting wands over them. Or that she would bump into Austin Goldman in one of the several terrible bookstore/candy stores, that carried none of the books he represented, a fact that wouldn't bother him, because he didn't represent bestsellers. He convinced editors they were buying a piece of the future, a gem of great literature, worth more for what it would snowball into over decades than any book that sold like hotcakes for six weeks but fell off the charts once people got around to actually reading it.

Allison had sent the famous writer's girlfriend a story she thought might be expanded into a novel and she'd brought printed copies in her carry-on in case she ran into Goldman or one of the famous writer's editors. She didn't know who she might see, here in Detroit, or seated together on the same plane, but she was ready for her chance meeting. She was surprised she hadn't heard back from the famous writer's girlfriend. She fully expected to be selected as the winner of her little contest and to be the one to be given the famous writer's last book, which she would milk for all it was worth. She'd tweet out lines from his book that would go viral, with a thousand faves, and she'd get an excerpt published at the *New Yorker*, where they'd let her read it for their podcast and would interview her afterwards, asking what he was like as a teacher and what invaluable lessons he'd passed on in his workshops. She was growing suspicious that maybe she wasn't the one picked to helm his book, but she couldn't imagine it going to anyone else. Maya Drake, maybe, but God, she hoped not. Maya got everything already as it was. Couldn't somebody somewhere see that she wasn't the only talented writer to come out of the Deep South Writers Workshop?

Scott handed her a Frappuccino as she flipped through the pages of her story to reassure herself that the famous writer's girlfriend was taking her time, and that she would announce the winner at some point during the reunion. She really did create a funny and vulnerable character who had a lot of her own mannerisms, which she was sure made her seem genuine. What would *she* do if Scott had been lured to the Caribbean to check out a new tax haven and he was abducted for ransom? She'd sell everything to get him back but would also feel liberated at his being gone. It was selfish, but the character in her story had an affair while he was being tortured by the islanders, and when she finally secured his release through contacts made via the man she'd cheated on him with—that was the irony, and irony was still hot no matter what anyone said—she didn't feel guilty but was weighted down with a sense of dread. She hated feeling indebted to him, and with him gone that feeling was gone. Yes, she had concern for his well-being, but these islanders only wanted money, there was never really any threat of him being harmed. When Scott handed her the Frappuccino—a small one, she forgot what they called that size, in a miniature paper coffee cup with a lid, a calculated decision made by Scott to try to balance the benefits of caffeine intake against the possibility that it may not be convenient for them to go to the bathroom once they were in the air—she flipped away from the sex scene, which involved her having her first orgasm solely through intercourse since early in her relationship with Scott, and she acted like she'd been reading the last pages when he walked up, the reunion with the Scott character where she realized how right he was for her, and how he gave her what she needed even if he wasn't the most interesting person or all that good in bed. Her last few sentences were lyrical as her character came to terms with the rightness of her life at that moment and her dalliance, though exciting and necessary, was now over, though it was truly necessary, especially as it brought all the right players together to bring about Scott's release, who was named Chaz in the story, who was also a tax lawyer, and who looked and acted exactly like Scott. She took the Frappuccino, glad to have her husband back, and glad that she'd written such a powerful story. International intrigue hadn't been her thing, but those books sold really well, and now that she'd written "The Girl on the Bus," she supposed that yes, international intrigue just might be her thing after all.

§

When Trisha A. and iMOL decided to share an Airbnb, Trisha told iMOL that she'd normally never share a room with a cis-gender white male, but that she knew he was enlightened enough and that there was no danger of miscommunication or misunderstanding between them. They'd been friends long enough that he knew her take on the patriarchy, and though he might not see himself as having any privileged role in society—in fact his iMOL persona was steadily dismantling *any* binary power structures—he was willing to admit that his masculinity, and his whiteness had made things easier for him over the years in ways he had never been expected to apologize for, though he did apologize, most often in the private conversations he'd had with Trisha A. during their Google Hangouts. If there were someone else he could trust with such information iMOL would admit that he had a crush on Trisha A, always had, and though he was sure there was no hope of them ever hooking up, she had trusted him enough that when they were drunk or high together in the one-bedroom apartment of the church secretary who let the place out through Airbnb, he hoped she would feel comfortable enough around him that she'd hang out with him in her underwear, or maybe even with no top at all, because she'd let it be known in articles and blog posts that a woman should have the right to go topless without harassment at any event, whether she was breastfeeding or not, whether there were children or not, whether it was a protest or a walk in the sun, and he seconded her belief in that right, and hoped it would one day come to pass in his presence, where he could admire her courage and her progressive politics, which would also be burned into his memory for later recollection.

The church secretary told them she mostly rented out her place for people who came to town for football games and that she was in the habit of keeping the place more clean during football season, which this was not, and so she was sorry, but when Trisha said she'd flown in from New York, the church secretary nodded as if she already knew this from Trisha's tattoos, piercings, and as she explained "Gothic" appearance, which also made the church secretary more at ease, since someone who lived in New York was probably used to a messy apartment.

Trisha explained that she and iMOL were writers with a moderate Internet readership and they were in town because a very important writer who lived in Petal had died, maybe she'd heard of him? But she had not, and she added that she had a cousin who wrote books that another cousin did the illustrations for, and they were kind of like Harry Potter books, only different. iMOL said it was the "different" part that mattered most and they all agreed, and they stood there with nothing else to say to each other, until the church secretary left, and Trisha fired up the coffee machine, with the intention of making coffee with the expensive coffee beans she'd brought, her one indulgence, except she soon realized the church secretary didn't have a coffee grinder. Of course she didn't. And instead of drinking the Folger's she found in the pantry, she was going to have to cope with her mid-day fatigue and caffeine withdrawal, though she was so glad to see iMOL in person again, that she kissed him right on the lips, except he let his palm slide down to cup her ass, and it was so slick and subtle she could hardly believe it was happening. She was a victim of misunderstanding and in order not to acknowledge this she suggested they go looking for a café, since Petal must have gotten a Starbucks by now. And iMOL agreed, and he recognized his error, and he blushed, though he also chose not to acknowledge the misunderstanding, because he didn't want to admit his place in the rape culture, and he also secretly hoped that maybe she'd come around, and in that case the message he'd sent by caressing her ass was precisely the right one, and he'd have been *the man* in this situation for not being too chicken to make a move.

§

Trent always imagined he would return to campus under different circumstances. He used to daydream that he'd been invited back to read, something he knew had happened for Maya Drake, the kind of milestone for a writer that meant more than any award, going back to where he'd begun and his mentor showing him off in front of the new crowd. Of course it hadn't happened for Trent. He'd written better books than Allison or Maya, but no one knew. He could hardly get agents to look at them. He sent off to contests only to Google around and learn that someone the judge had shared a panel with at a conference two years ago was selected as the winner. He sent to small presses, the handful with open submission periods, also with no luck. Trent toiled in obscurity driven by the deeply felt notion that his work was valuable and good.

Spring was his favorite season in Mississippi, and it came early, heating up in February, with everything in bloom, every bush alive with color. The crepe myrtles and magnolias drew the eye and teemed with bees and by mid-afternoon the air became heavy with heat. Trent was glad they hadn't planned this for any later in the year, when it would be unbearably hot. He remembered dripping with sweat anytime he walked from his apartment door to his car, or from his car into another building. One minute outside in a Mississippi summer was all it took. He supposed Southerners were acclimated, because people lived here long before air conditioning, and as mild as the winters were he also remembered times when he felt chilled to the bone. He parked on the edge of campus, in the visitor parking lot, and he walked toward Nathan Bedford Forrest Hall, a walk that automatically put him in a meditative mood. When he was in the program, this walk would have had him mulling over what he might say about another writer's story, or it would have him steeling himself for the petty criticism directed at his own story. He wondered if his writing had been as good as it was these days if they'd still respond to him with the same barbs and insults. He was pretty sure they would. Because there was no such thing as an objective assessment of literature, and since they all knew him and had all, at some point, at some party, or as he sat in his parked car on campus, seen him puffing on a spliff, the subjective reactions to his writing were doubly true. He realized that maybe workshopping again was a bad idea, that they weren't going to be able to enjoy his work any more than he would enjoy theirs, though he hoped that they'd gotten better too, and he really was rooting for them. He wanted them to be good and for them all to simply be supportive, which seemed the reasonable way to go about the workshop, even if it wasn't in service of art. There was very little chance of that approach coming to fruition here, since the dead writer had always expected them to check their feelings at the door and to be vigilant in rooting out the flaws of the narratives they pored over, with the assumption that the writer being workshopped had the skill to smooth over the flaws and could also communicate a subtle but clear intention.

By the time Trent had entered Nathan Bedford Forrest Hall, his heart was racing. Which was ridiculous, because the famous writer wouldn't be there. He was only meeting with Lydia so she could give him a key to one of the dorm rooms.

Lydia seemed genuinely pleased to see Trent. She was in the enviable position of only knowing the students as people and never having to trouble herself with their writing. She introduced Trent to Sparrow Walsh, who was out of her office to greet any of the famous writer's former students who would be arriving that day. Trent smiled and shook her hand with a nod of recognition that suggested he was familiar with her work. He wasn't. And he tried to hide the fact that he was disappointed with how young she was. If he'd been lucky enough to place a few more stories in the right magazines, he could be at some university with a job like hers. It was hard not to feel, given the writing he'd been doing lately, that he *should* have a job like hers.

Lydia led him back out and to another part of campus, where the tall blocky dorms were. He'd always avoided that part of campus. Lydia gave him a temporary ID with a photo of him she'd gotten online and she also gave him a key. She introduced him to the guard who sat at a desk near the elevators and she explained that the guard may not be there when he came and went, since the kids were required to vacate over spring break, but he would still be asked to sign in or sign out and note the time on the ledger. He was only here to drop off his bag and to acquaint himself with the room, and then he was off to the famous writer's house where he would meet with the famous writer's girlfriend. He had read the book and his head was filled with it. He was sure it was publishable but it was also an unconventional book, and while he suspected that maybe the famous writer had been up to something important that he hadn't quite gleaned, he was quite sure the book wouldn't make a splash, and he was going to have to tell her. Whatever plans she had made for the royalties, she should dial them down. It wasn't at all like his other work, and it was the kind of book that might go to a small publisher, and in which case she shouldn't expect to make money.

Lydia brought him into the room, which had a desk, a bunk, and a small closet, and she indicated the view. They were ten stories up and could see quite a lot of the campus, and the town. If he had come here as an undergraduate and had lived in the room by himself, that view would have informed his writing. He'd have spent a lot of time looking out that window as he searched for the right words to the stories that he suspected would have turned out differently.

"Are you coming to the party?" Trent asked Lydia before she snuck away.

"No, that's for you all," she said. "I'll be at the memorial service. And I'll be in the offices during the week if you need anything."

"You don't get to enjoy spring break?"

"I get a week where I can finally get work done because there aren't fifty kids trying to get out of Dr. So-and-so's English class."

"Not naming any names?"

"You could probably guess," she said.

He could guess. There were a few of them on the literature side of the department who were exceedingly strict for no good reason. Thanks to them a lot of the undergraduates graduated from the university with an experience of literature that left a bad taste. These graduates would forever see themselves as incapable of appreciating literature, and they might go the rest of their lives without ever giving it a try again. The English professors blamed our TV culture and a university that put most of its money in sports and polymer science, but Trent felt that some of these same teachers, who had devoted their lives to literature, had also ruined it for a lot of young people, by trying to claim literature as their own. They created an environment that sapped all the joy out of literature. They had arrived at a place after decades of reading that they expected their young students to reach in one semester. Trent realized that these literature professors must be relieved that the famous writer had died. They weren't in his shadow anymore, which pretty much insured that they would impose themselves into the search for his replacement, and they might even work toward dismantling the Deep South Writers Workshop and *The Deep South Triannual*, and for the first time Trent realized that the death of the famous writer might mean that Lydia could lose her job. He didn't care too much about what happened to the program. It had been there for him and he was grateful, but there were so many writing programs these days that it wouldn't be all too tragic if it did fold. Except for Lydia. She'd always been kind to the students and found ways of minimizing the famous writer's reign of terror, and so he hoped the program would be spared for her sake.

"Thank you for everything, Lydia," Trent said, and he was alone in a dorm room for the first time since he was nineteen, which filled him with the irresistible urge to go buy weed. Of course, he didn't know anyone, and even if he did they'd be gone on spring break. He put the pillowcase on the pillow and the sheets on the bed. He lay on it to test the comfort and he stared out the window until he finally got up for fear that he might fall asleep. He took his book bag with his laptop in it, he locked up the room, and he headed back down the hallway where he saw Maya Drake and Sparrow Walsh coming toward him.

Sparrow let Maya into one of the dorm rooms in the same suite, and after Trent and Maya hugged, glad to see each other, Trent said, "I thought you'd be staying at the Double Tree."

"Too expensive," Maya said, and Trent was surprised. She had successful books. One was even optioned for a movie. She had a good teaching job at Pitt. Surely, she could afford a stay at the Double Tree. Though a room was a room and staying in the dorms was considerably cheaper. Maya's view was equally as grand, though at a ninety-degree-angle from Trent's, and she also had the advantage of being able to see down into the bowl of the football stadium. If there were a game, they could sit in her room and drink and smoke spliffs and watch the whole spectacle for free.

Because of the workshop they'd planned, the first moments of meeting any of the other writers again was going to be odd. Because they had read each other's stories, and while they would save their critiques for the workshop, each would want some sign that the story had been a success. Maya had read Trent's story and Trent had read Maya's, and they were both thinking about that, and they both wanted to know what the other thought, though neither would bring it up, and Maya had always had a confidence about what she was doing where she didn't really need validation, but she still felt good about it when it came. Trent got the feeling that Maya wanted to be alone but he wanted to tell her about the famous writer's book, so he loitered. Sparrow loitered too. It was obvious she had read Maya's books and looked up to her and wanted to be her friend. Eventually, Maya kicked them both out, but as soon as Sparrow was gone down the hall, Trent knocked on Maya's door.

She answered, tired from the flight and exasperated at seeing

Trent again after she'd just gotten rid of him.

"I've read his book," Trent said. "His girlfriend gave it to me."

"Can I see it?"

"She made me promise not to show anyone. It was one of her conditions."

"So?"

"It's really different."

"Different how?"

"He's less serious. There's more of a universal view. He's got a lot more characters, and different kinds of characters. Some of it is funny."

"No!"

"I'm telling you."

"Why do you think she picked you?" Maya said, and she backed away from the door to let him come into her room so they could talk.

He sat at the desk and she sat on the bare mattress of the bottom bunk.

"What do you mean?" He said. "We all sent her stories."

"I was emailing him," Maya said. "We stayed in contact. If he was working on a book, he would have told me."

"He wrote it several years ago," Trent said. "He was saving it."

"He did tell me his girlfriend had worked on a book."

"*She* was a writer?"

"She was one of his students."

"I didn't know that. What are you suggesting?"

"I think you know what I'm suggesting."

"But why would she do that? What could she gain?"

"She gets Austin Goldman to sell the novel she wrote and she sits back while everyone in the literary establishment goes gaga over her book. And then maybe a few years down the road she spills the beans and makes fools out of them, exposes the whole façade and her book starts selling all over again."

"That's pretty dastardly. You really think she's capable of that?"

"We are all capable of that."

"I'm not," Trent offered.

"Okay," Maya agreed. "Everyone but you is capable of that."

"*You* would do that?"

"If I didn't already have an agent, and I had tried, and no one was biting, fuck yeah I'd do it."

"I don't know," Trent said. "You don't have any proof."

"There is a way to prove it," Maya said. "You said yourself it was really different."

"That's not proof."

"You could prove it through linguistic analysis."

"Matched vocabulary?"

"Does it sound like him or does it sound like her?"

"They were intimate for years and years," Trent said. "They are going to naturally be interested in the same things. And they will eventually start to sound like each other."

"If I were you," Maya said. "I would try to find out more about this manuscript before I put my name on it."

"You think I'm gullible?" Trent said. "You think she picked me for reasons that had nothing to do with my writing but because she imagined I was someone she could trick?"

"That's exactly what I think."

"You haven't seen my work in a long time," Trent said. "And if

I'm so persuadable why does she need me anyway?"

"The main thing," Maya said, "is to get someone talking about the book and to keep it out of Goldman's hands for as long as possible. Get him salivating over it so that he's already primed his contacts, and when he finally gets it, he goes through with the publishing deal as quickly as possible."

"If she wanted to create buzz she should have picked Allison," Trent said. "She's got like twenty thousand Twitter followers."

"Allison would turn it to her own advantage," Maya said. "You won't."

"Why won't I?"

"Because you don't know how. You're a *great* writer Trent but you've never learned to sell it. You have to be able to convince someone else its good and you were too imbued with integrity to do that. You always focused on the writing itself, but the writing alone will never get you anywhere."

"I've tried to sell. I send my stuff out."

"You send it out cold. You haven't made contacts. You haven't scratched any backs. And you would never in a million years kiss ass."

"I would kiss ass if the writer was good. If they deserved to have their ass kissed."

"That's a small number," Maya said. "And those writers are doing just fine. Kissing the ass of someone who doesn't need or want to have their ass kissed is worse than not kissing ass at all."

"That's how I feel anyway."

"You need to get over it," Maya said. "You've got a real opportunity here, but don't promote the book if you can't be sure it's his. Calling her out is just as good or better for you than doing what she wants."

"My book is better anyway."

"What did you just say?"

"My book," Trent repeated. "It's better."

"That attitude has got to go," Maya told him.

"It's true."

"Believing it doesn't make it true."

"I know it. I'm sure of it."

"This is exactly what I'm talking about," Maya said. "It doesn't matter how good your book is. In the eyes of the people who make careers, you'll never be as good as Colonel Kurtz and it's because of who he was. He was part of a movement and he affected change."

"There aren't movements anymore."

"No, there aren't. Nor will there be."

"I missed my time?"

"It wasn't your time, but yes, it's late in the game."

"The fame game?"

"You knew what it was," Maya said. "Just be happy you're a good writer. You'll never get rich from it, but it is worth something."

"Why are we even here?"

"To pay our respects to the guy."

"He was a dick to us. Not to you. You were his pet. But to the rest of us. You saw how he was."

"He didn't believe in coddling us."

"He coddled you."

"He criticized my stories plenty of times."

"Not in the same way. Not even close."

"You may not want to hear this," Maya said, "but he knew you had talent and he thought you were wasting it."

"Wasting it how?"

"The stories didn't match your potential. And you were always high."

"That has nothing to do with it."

"I'm only telling you what he told me."

"So if I had quit smoking pot and handed in better stories I'd be where you are today?"

"Of course not. Mostly, you need to quit being so haughty and to kiss a little ass."

"When did you kiss ass?"

"I kissed a lot of ass."

"I liked your books," Trent said. "I really liked your books."

"Thanks," she said.

If he were honest he'd have said he liked the first fifty pages of her books. They kind of fell apart after that. He suspected that she worked on the books from the beginning each time, so with each successive pass the beginning got worked over quite a lot more, with the chapters toward the end glaring with poor choices and inexcusably loose prose. He blamed the process, where an agent could sell a book with a good title and good opening chapters. And he blamed the editors, who should have worked with her more to give her books better endings. And he blamed himself, for being such a purist when the novel itself was a flawed form. It was rare that even the best novelists could produce a masterpiece. Generally, the names we all know, the writers in the pantheon, they each had their one great book while the others they wrote tended to demonstrate their competence while falling short of their best work again and again.

"I really do need to rest before this party," Maya said as a way of kicking him out again.

"I'm going over there now."

"Are you going to ask her?"

"If she really did what you think she did, she'd never admit it."

"Dr. Cleary's the linguist in the department. He could do an analysis."

"I don't know him."

"They hired him after we left. He'd be honest and objective. He seems like a good guy."

"I promised not to show it to anyone."

"That was under the pretense that it was really his book."

"I never doubted it until you brought it up. I'll keep this Cleary guy in mind."

§

At the front desk of the Double Tree Hotel a college student in an ill-fitting green polo with the Hilton logo stitched above his name tag was explaining the amenities, the same as he would to any traveler, though Austin Goldman was well-accustomed to hotel service beyond what Petal could provide. In his gold wire-rimmed glasses and his white linen suit he tried not to look bored but the kid continued to talk, when from behind him Holly Rorsch gave him an over-enthusiastic greeting and he turned and bent down to kiss her cheek. Holly was short and wore her dark hair in a bob. Like Goldman she'd stayed with the same look for ages. She was girlish, though in her fifties, and her stature contradicted her influence among publishers. Her glasses were low on her nose, with a librarian's chain to catch them should they fall. They shifted and she pushed them back up her nose.

"I didn't know if I'd see anyone from the biz," Goldman said.

"I was already scheduled to pay a visit to the program and the new girl told me to come anyway."

"Yes. What's her name?"

"It's something birdy."

"Finch?"

"Sparrow, I think."

"Unfortunate."

"Could have worked if she were Native American."

"She's not even a little?"

"Oh, who knows? How have you been? I read about your latest 'very nice deal'."

"Which one?" Goldman said and they laughed. "Not as nice as that Colin Becker book."

"Have you read it?" Holly said. "I hear it's awful."

"He sent it to me," Goldman said. "I wasn't going to read one thousand pages."

"Neither will the people who buy it."

"It's never going to pay out. I don't know how Elaine got so much. I mean, I do, but there are ten books that won't get published this year because of that thing."

"Was it really so bad? There must be something."

"Becker is capable. He can write character, but I just didn't *care*. I passed on it."

"You passed on one-hundred-and-fifty thou-."

"I don't care. I am happy not to be associated with it."

"Good for Elaine, though, right?"

"The book is a dis-service to humanity. But Elaine will have writers breaking down her door. She can stop reading queries, that's for sure."

"I can't," Holly said. "I'm afraid I'll miss something."

"You won't."

"Elaine got Becker from his query."

"We'd all already passed on it. That's already his story. Supposed to be inspirational for writers: Colin Becker's book gets a seven-figure deal after thirty agents pass on it. That's all we need is more writers bolstered by rejection. And that's why I don't look at queries."

"Sorry about the Minimalist."

"There was a rumor that he was dying," Goldman said, "but killed by a car? That was unexpected."

"Could happen to anyone."

"It wasn't supposed to happen to him."

"Is the estate settled? What's going to happen?"

"It all goes to a girlfriend."

"And the new book?" Holly said. "I'm assuming you've read it."

Goldman was used to keeping his cards close, and Holly Rorsch gave the impression that she knew more about the famous writer's unpublished novel than he did.

"What book?"

"Ha ha," Holly said. "Are you being coy? There's a book. Haven't you talked to this girlfriend?"

"Yes, of course. But I haven't read it."

"I should have kept my mouth shut and that book could have been mine."

"Is that why you came? To swoop down on his legacy?"

"No, darling," Holly said. "I'll leave that to you."

§

After they had checked in, Allison found reasons to hang out in the lobby. She kept taking sips from the water fountain. She acted interested in the tourism brochures. Scott understood that she was trying to provoke a chance meeting with Goldman. He explained that Goldman might not even stay at the Double Tree.

"Where else would he stay?" Allison whispered.

"I don't know," Scott said. "New Orleans."

She hadn't thought of that. It was entirely possible. Would be much more his style. There wasn't enough opulence or decadence in Petal. The bus boy led them to the elevator and up to their room as Allison stole glances back over her shoulder.

Once they were alone in their room, Scott looked up the minibar prices in the room service menu and he was immediately sorry he hadn't picked up a bottle. He hadn't been with Allison in a hotel room in quite a while, they had some time to kill before this party, and he wanted sex. He took off his clothes, slowly, so she might take a hint, but she went over to the door to look out the peephole.

"Any literary agents out there?"

"Shut up," she said.

He nuzzled behind her and kissed her on the neck, but she swatted at him.

"I'm going to take a shower to freshen up. Care to join me?"

"I'm good," she said, which indicated a wall he wasn't going to be scaling this afternoon.

He took out a mini-bottle of champagne from the mini-fridge and popped it open, which startled her and she turned and smiled, a fool for champagne. He poured the bottle into two water glasses, all there was, and he proposed a toast, "To your dead mentor. You are finally free of him."

"I'll never be free of him," she sighed, and she slumped into a chair. They clinked glasses and she downed the whole glass, which was encouraging. He could move her onto white wine and might get what he wanted after all. He pulled up a chair next to her, pulled off her shoes and massaged her feet. She lay back and closed her eyes with a smile, pleased at everything in that moment. Until a stray hand made its way up her leg and she bolted upright.

"I am not sleeping with you."

"We could have some sex."

"I'm tired."

"It's a good lead-in for a nap."

"You know I'm a bad napper. I'll wake up groggy."

"We have coffee. This party is going to go late. A nap might be a good thing."

Someone was heard talking in the hallway as they passed and Allison pointed at the door. "That could have been Goldman."

"You'll see him soon enough."

"Why haven't I heard from this girlfriend? She probably picked Maya because Maya wrote that fucking essay. I should have written an essay."

"You still could."

"No, she ruined it."

"We could take a bath."

"Will you leave me alone if I fuck you?"

"I will absolutely leave you alone if you fuck me."

"You're not going to try to fuck me twice?"

"Twice is nice."

"I'll do it once. And you better be quick."

"Deal."

§

There was a landscaping crew mowing the famous writer's grass in preparation for the party. The house was a Victorian with a large porch. Not a humongous house but the kind of place Trent knew he would never be able to afford. His teacher was able to live like that because of his writing. There were so many other writers who were as good, Trent included, but he saw himself more likely to be one of the guys pushing a mower. He nodded 'hello' to them and went to the door.

The girlfriend answered and Trent was surprised that she was younger than he was. She'd dated the famous writer for over a decade and Maya had said she'd been a graduate student, so she had to be in her thirties, which wasn't young-young, but comparatively she was quite young, and would have been in her twenties when she and the famous writer started going out. She was attractive. Trent would have said she was 'cute,' but he had expected her to be more of a bombshell. As his books made clear, the famous writer had a thing for blondes, which this girlfriend was not. Her voice was musical, though, and Trent understood the attraction. He did not restrain himself from looking her up-and-down as he followed her into the house.

They sat in the kitchen and she poured two cups of coffee. The kitchen was cool and bright and Trent imagined the famous writer working at this table, though he knew he hadn't been writing these past several years.

"So...?"

"About the book?" Trent said. The way she was looking at him made him feel like he had to choose his words carefully, because it might be her book she'd asked him to read. "It was a surprise. It felt young."

"How so?"

"Well he's not a Minimalist anymore, is he?"

"I know," she said. "Isn't it great? There's no restraints."

"He used to say that the restraint forced one to be more creative. That the art was more pure."

"Not since I'd known him."

"I guess I don't know how to talk about him with you. I don't know your history together and I don't want to say anything that might be inappropriate."

"You won't offend me."

"Something I'm curious about," Trent began, "was that he was always really hard on us. And so how did that, for you anyway, turn into attraction?"

"I'm a masochist."

"Oh..."

"I'm joking," the girlfriend said. "He did all that for show. The famous writer bit. Once you got to know him, he was a sweetheart."

"The old atheist?"

"He believed in things."

"Like what?"

"Coincidence. Luck. A psychological connection. The innate goodness of dogs."

"And Truth? And art?"

"I think he was tired of it."

"Some of us who bought into it weren't."

"I know. This Allison character is insufferable."

"She's a friend of mine. Was her story that bad?"

"I didn't read it. I didn't have to. I looked her up online and there were all these author interviews where she blathered on about the writing process and suffering."

"Writing is painful for some people."

"Then why do they do it? No one is making her do it."

"I think you know why."

"You can be good at something without having to be famous."

"You're a writer, right?"

"I was."

"You quit?"

"I wasn't going to write if he wasn't writing. It didn't seem fair."

"Why not?"

"I think he wasn't writing because of me. We were happy together. He'd changed. He wanted to spend time with me instead of sentences."

"It's understandable, but one *can* do both."

"The time he spent with me where he wasn't writing was time I spent with him where I wasn't writing."

"You're young. You can start again. I mean not right away but eventually."

"Quitting was easy. The Truth and art shit is a drag."

"I can't quit. I don't want to quit."

"I feel like I have a better perspective on it now that I'm not in it. I can see the B.S. more easily—like all the B.S. that Allison girl spews."

"Where did the book come from?"

"I told you. His laptop. From years ago."

"You're sure it's his?"

"What are you suggesting?"

"Maybe a student sent it to him to look at or something. I don't know."

"Nonsense. I remember when he was working on it. I didn't know he'd finished or that he'd been hanging on to it. What did you think? Is it good?"

"It's great. I liked it a lot. It's not commercial but not trying to be literary. No one who read it blind would ever guess it was him. Now that I've met you I feel like there's some of you in there."

"Of course there is."

"Is that why you didn't want to read it?"

"Partly. It's just too soon. If I don't read it there's still a part of him that I have left. Once I read it he's all gone. It's his last book."

"Do you think it's also painful because you quit writing? That it's close to you but also not yours?"

"I've been at peace with quitting writing for a long time. He took the place of writing for me and being with him was better than being alone."

"You're afraid to be alone again?"

"I'm afraid of being with him again and having it end again."

"Listen, I know you might feel funny about it, and you may not have anything to submit, but we're all going to get together and workshop. You're welcome to come, but you'd have to turn in a story."

"I have some old stuff, but that doesn't seem right."

"Write something new."

"When will I find the time?"

"Stay up late. Get up early. It's what we do."

"I was thinking you could write a preface for his book," the girlfriend said. "That way you'd get a publication credit and some money."

"Wow," Trent said. "Thanks."

"I can't write anything for a workshop," the girlfriend said. "Who are we kidding here? I'm not in the right state of mind."

"There's a four-hour visitation window tomorrow that's just for the students. That's when we're going to workshop. If you sent something out tonight not everyone would read it but some of us would."

"With him in the room?"

"It was the easiest way to get everyone together. We'll have the space. Having him there seemed right."

"I'm going to have to pass. It's just too weird."

"I know it sounds weird, but if he kept you from writing this could be your rebirth."

"He didn't keep me from writing, not in a bad way. We were happy. I'm going to need time to get over that first. And if I don't write again, the world will be fine with one less writer."

"Of course that's true," Trent said. "But I'm also still religious about it. I haven't let go. I can't."

"It was easier than you'd think. All you need is someone to replace it."

§

After lunching at the Hub City Grill, the establishment where Allison thought she'd most likely bump into Goldman, she dragged Scott to the campus library, where she wandered the stacks looking for her books, which weren't there, but Maya's were, and she reeled with the possibilities about who was ordering books. Was it a librarian or someone from the English Department, or even the famous writer himself? The last was the most upsetting possibility though she didn't imagine Kurtz spending time here in the library. At any rate it was a glaring oversight. How could they not have the books of an illustrious graduate of the writing program? Had they known about her but thought she wasn't literary enough? She suspected that if they went down to the public library, which was one tenth the size, someone there had ordered her books. She could walk into any library at random and supposed there was a fifty-fifty chance they'd have one of her books. But her alma mater couldn't be bothered? She walked the stacks of the contemporary fiction, some of these same books the copies she'd read when she was absorbing literature day and night, and she recognized each by the pastel cloth library binding. She had spent countless hours as a graduate student alone with these very books. She still often spent her days with a book, thanks to Scott, but she didn't go to libraries much anymore. Friends would send her advance copies when they wanted a blurb. Her agent sent copies of the books from the other writers she represented and editors would send copies of the other books they'd published. And when something she wanted to read didn't fall into one of these categories, which was often enough, Amazon would send it to her thanks to one-click online shopping. There were writers who saw Amazon as the end of civilization, but she wasn't one of them. They may have put bookstores out of business but she had often lived in towns with shitty bookstores, and Amazon made it possible for her to be as well-read as she was, and it was always wonderful to get books in the mail. She hadn't transitioned to Kindle, however, which was even more immediate. As long as there was Wi-Fi, the book could arrive as soon as one had the notion to buy it. She fell into the middle of the debate on electronic books. She recognized that cutting down trees to publish more books was wasteful, but she also loved the feel and smell of a book, which an article she had read identified as the binding glue. To say it like that sounded funny, that one of the things she loved most about reading was the smell of binding glue, but there it was, and this was true. Scott stayed near and pretended to look at the titles of the books. She knew he didn't know any of these authors, not even the more famous ones, and once she was overcome with the injustice of not being here in these stacks, which she'd worked for, and which she deserved, she took Scott by the hand and led him to the elevator. They rode down to the front desk, where a woman who was not a student but a member of the library faculty waited for her question.

Allison told the librarian that she needed her to order some books and she rattled off the titles of her own, titles she'd come to love like children. One of the titles was suggested by her agent and one by an editor, and she didn't like them at first, but they grew on her as she got mostly favorable reviews, and there would be the title of her book in the title of the review, and she was there too, in her author photo. She loved it so much, mostly because she'd been lucky enough not to get a really bad review yet, and each review made her feel slightly more famous.

The librarian typed the titles of Allison's books into her computer and she did so slowly, so that Allison lost her patience and snapped, "You don't have these books, and you need to order them."

She spoke much too loud for library etiquette, even during spring break when there were fewer patrons than usual.

"We don't have these books," the librarian confirmed, "but I can help you with an acquisition request. It probably would be faster to get them through interlibrary loan. With an acquisition they may not be on the shelf until next semester. We have to order them, then catalog them, then bind them, then put them on the shelf…"

"I don't want them through interlibrary loan. I don't want to read them. I've read them. I wrote them."

"That's fabulous," the librarian said. "I'm so happy for you."

"It's been a few years," Allison said. "I expected you would already have them."

"We don't order all the books," the librarian explained. "For something like that, someone would have had to make an acquisition request. If you have your library card I can pull up the form and get you started."

"I don't have a library card."

"Do you know your number?"

"I don't have a card. I'm alumni."

"I see," the librarian said. "Well an acquisition request has to come from a student or a faculty member."

"*You're* a faculty member."

"I can't do it though. I could get in trouble."

Allison was red in the face and Scott stood next to her, blank and calm. He'd seen her like this before and he knew not to intervene or he would make things worse.

"Do you know someone who could do an acquisition for you?"

She didn't, but she would soon enough. They were going to a party in a few hours where she'd see some faculty members and some current students. She would have the titles and ISBN numbers written down for them, and one of them would do this for her, but she was embarrassed it had come to this, because she shouldn't have had to have been the one to ask.

Allison didn't feel like explaining all of this, and so she said, "Thank you for nothing," and she stormed back out the automated doors.

"You could have been nicer to that librarian," Scott said once they were outside.

"She wasn't doing her job."

"It's not her job to know every book that comes out."

"They did a profile on me in the *Petal Advocate*. How could she have missed it?"

"It's probably a budget thing where they have to pick and choose. Maybe the profile came out after they'd blown all the money and then they forgot."

"It's not a budget thing," Allison said. She had been rude to the librarian who, in that moment, had been a representative of the forces working against her—first it had been her parents, who thought she should have gone into real estate like they had, then it was the famous writer who, though generally more supportive than he was of the other students, still made her feel like shit after workshopping a story, and there were the end of year "best of" lists that she'd only ever gotten onto three of, and she'd never been nominated for an award, or picked by Oprah, or picked by Barnes and Noble. She wasn't even picked by this stupid librarian. And she was furious at Scott, who didn't know anything about books or libraries, and suddenly she was screaming at him, "Did you see how many fucking shitty books they have in there?"

"I didn't know which ones were shitty."

"A lot of them. Most of them."

"Someone will order your books," Scott said and the episode was over for him. She tended to want to hang on to her anger longer, but his general reasonableness in these situations made her feel stupid, which made her angry for different reasons, though it was a less-intense anger that would subside after ten or twenty minutes of him acting like nothing important had happened, because to him it hadn't been important, and while he was capable of empathy he was also just as likely to be emotionally unavailable. She was traumatized that no one at the Deep South Writers Workshop had ordered her books. Meanwhile, Scott had already put it out of his mind.

When they were back in the car, he said, "Is there anything else you want to do while we're here before we go to this party? Or should we go back to the hotel?"

She could think of nothing else she wanted to do, but she also didn't want to go to the hotel because it would remind him that he wanted sex and she'd already given him that today.

"I want to see the cemetery. We passed it coming into town. Go back out toward the airport."

At the front gate of the cemetery there was a statue of Nathan Bedford Forrest on a rearing horse, his sword drawn, and she couldn't remember if it meant he'd died in battle or if there was also some special iconography for a Klansman, but the statue was creepy enough without knowing who he'd been, because the sculptor had given him pupils, which meant drilling deep holes into his eyes. He was surrounded by the Confederate dead who had the same thin alabaster stones as the other veterans, with the name of the war carved below the name of the deceased, and as they rolled down the drive they drove past the wreckage of the Civil War, WWI, WWII, Korea, Vietnam, as well as a handful of casualties from Iraq and Afghanistan, which surprised her, and soon they were surrounded by civilians, who were spaced out in sprawling sections, with the newer ones in sections that only allowed flat stones flush with the ground, so they were easier to mow. And in one of these sections, she saw a backhoe parked next to a pile of dirt and a tent and folding chairs that had been set up for the famous writer's ceremony tomorrow. She told Scott to park, and she walked over there, and since there was no one around, she climbed into the famous writer's hole and she lay down on her back looking up, hoping to get a glimpse of the view from eternity, but there was that stupid tent above her, so she closed her eyes, Scott yammering on about something once he'd finally caught up with her.

"Please shut up," she told him, so he sat in one of the folding chairs and waited. She listened to the silence and emptied her mind of any thoughts. It took a few minutes, but she arrived at serenity and she wondered why she hadn't done this more often, not climbing into open graves but meditating, which was supposed to cure everything. She would be less prone to anger, she'd care less about not being famous, and she'd be more mentally acute when she needed to be. She was at peace, for a moment, with a body to her right and a body to her left, as she lay in the hole intended for her dead mentor and listened to the quiet of the old cemetery in the afternoon. She supposed the backhoe had a special shovel that was the exact width of a grave, and she sat up and looked at the clean lines of the dirt walls around her. As easy as it was for her to jump down into this hole, she realized that without Scott to help her back out she would have been stuck. She'd have only gotten out by collapsing the walls, and that would have been a shame, especially if the cemetery crew hadn't noticed until the funeral goers arrived with their body that they'd have to place next to a collapsed hole until someone fixed it.

Scott lifted her out easily and said, "You okay?"

"There's a lot going on. I'm still processing, but I'll be fine. Thanks for coming along. You ready to meet some writers?"

"Sure, why not?"

§

iMOL hadn't been to a party in a long time and he was determined to make this one count. He wore the parachute pants he'd paid a ridiculously high price for on eBay. He suspected he was bidding against the Smithsonian, but he'd made a quick bid in the last seconds of the auction and the pants were shipped to him, bright magenta and in pristine condition, one of the zippers a near-match and obviously a replacement but this wasn't noticeable without close examination, and everyone at this party would be blown away. He was ready to make a splash. Of course he wasn't old enough to have ever experienced parachute pants in their natural habitat, but he was made well-aware of the lore around them, since he had pretty much grown up on the Internet.

Trisha A. wore a pastel summer dress that gave the impression she was trying to be ironic, since everything else about her was hard-edged and gothic. They held hands as they went into the party, with no boyfriend-girlfriend vibe about them, they were like European teenagers cruising the streets at night. Trisha had brought a Chablis, and iMOL had a top-shelf vodka. They had arrived fashionably late and they separated to mingle, iMOL moving to the table in the dining room where there was a platter of fruit and a platter of sliced cheeses. In separate groups around the table were some of the older writers, who would be able to guess that he was iMOL, and they had read "Internet Log 4419." Likewise, he had read their stories, and while he thought they labored in narrative structures that were obsolete, he loved them for it. They wrote their traditional *New Yorker* stories quite well and he could appreciate them the way he might appreciate a string quartet or a still-life painting. The other group who hovered around the cheeses were English professors from the literature side of the department. He knew two of them, from having taken their classes, and he suspected the others were either spouses or new hires. He nodded a 'hello' to the professor who gave him a 'B' in his Wallace Stevens seminar, though iMOL was pretty sure he'd handed in the best papers, and he suspected it had something to do with a grudge the Wallace Stevens professor had against the famous writer, and so any of the creative writers who took his classes could expect a 'B,' or worse. iMOL didn't intend to ever use his degree to teach, and so he didn't really care about the grade, and he didn't care about Wallace Stevens either, in the way one might feel nothing at all about a string quartet or a still-life painting.

The older alumni called him over and they introduced themselves, and one of the oldest writers in the group also happened to be a current student who told them his name was Jeff Tequila, which was a close enough approximation to his real name that it was what he went by in these situations, and he told them what Bobby Knight's workshops had been like lately. He said there was an atmosphere where Bobby Knight encouraged the suck-ups, but now that he was dead, the suck-ups had nothing to show for their groveling, no Henfield nominations, no artists' colony recommendations, no internships, no letters of introduction. None of the suck-ups had even showed up at the party. He suspected they took their spring break in Gulf Shores, to stare out at the ocean, sip daiquiris and reassess their life choices. The current student editor of *Deep South Triannual* was on the back-porch smoking cigarettes if anyone wanted to slip her a story, though they were on hiatus, and they also had an official policy of not publishing alumni, except that they did it all the time. The interim director of the program was here somewhere though she might be mistaken for a student. The rumor was that she was on her way out. She would teach workshops for another year or two, but unless she also published a book in that time she wasn't going to get tenure and she'd be back out on the job market to compete alongside her own graduating students.

The famous writer's girlfriend was in the kitchen, where the famous writer used to hold court. He was fond of smoking cigars until his girlfriend would chew him out and make him puff on the back porch. "It's *my* house!" he would say, and she would shout back, "Get it out of here!" There would be cigars tonight at some point, in his honor, with even the women smoking them like George Eliot as they giddily drew the comparison and chided each other that they were like George Eliot. For Jeff Tequila, it was strange to be in his house, at one of his parties, without him there. The rest of them had been away long enough that the nostalgia of place welled up in them and it was fun to be at a party in his house again, and they hadn't seen him in so long that his absence wasn't all too unusual. If Maya Drake had written the scene, the ghost of the famous writer would be walking from room to room, unsettled that no one could see him, with none of the suck-ups coming up to him to tell him how much they loved his books, no poking at the students with a newly mean thing he hadn't yet thought to say about their writing that being suddenly confronted with their faces brought out in him, no playful arguments with his girlfriend about how he could behave how he pleased in his own home, even with people over, even with sensitive people over, and drinking until he went upstairs to pass out in bed with the party winding down but likely to continue at least another hour. Maya would have written his ghost weary and alone, though trying to entertain himself, which he might occasionally find success at. He would pretend to answer the phone and he'd make animated expressions as he pretended to listen to whomever on the line, or he'd walk with giant shoes and try to hold onto a bouquet of balloons that would get away. As Maya wrote him he would be an accomplished mime working for attention but never breaking through to the party-goers.

In the kitchen, Trisha A. made new friends with the conversation-starter she used on everyone: "Who was it who ruined you? Who do you blame for getting you into this dead-end literary writer game?" And no one had said the famous writer.

Allison said, "Flannery O'Connor," which brought smiles all around. This was the best response. O'Connor was inimitable, and her sense of humor and the strangeness of the South that she satirized was hers alone, coupled with the searing heat of an ever-present divinity. O'Connor died young, so her output was limited, but one might never tire of her.

"Didn't you grow up in Ohio?" Trent said.

"I expected Mississippi to be like that," Allison said. "I was infatuated with the South."

"It was still like that in some ways. In pockets."

The beauty of Trisha's icebreaker was that no one was expected to write like the author who had turned them on to literature, yet it might inform the story they'd handed in to workshop, at least a little. Could they ever truly get away from their influences?

Scott leaned close to Allison. He never let her get too far from him in these situations. He could handle a party, but a party of writers and professors was bound to make him feel dumb. He knew the question wasn't intended for him, as someone who had not devoted his life to writing and literature. But if he were to reply he would give high marks to the first story he had read all the way through, assigned in an English class when he was in high school, "The Most Dangerous Game," and he carried the lesson of it with him even today. Because out in the jungle, hunting big game, one might expect a lion, or a hippo to be the most dangerous, but no, as the story made clear as its double-meaning was revealed, *man* was the most dangerous game. The corner of Scott's lip rose into a half-smile as he thought about it. He remembered being blown away by the story, and when he talked about it in class his teacher, Ms. Brock, who wore short skirts and tall boots, was so happy with him in a way he recognized now as slightly condescending, but that felt like genuine approval at the time. Scott had missed his chance to enter the conversation and that was probably for the best. He didn't have a drink yet, and he didn't know what to do with his hands.

Trent revealed a love for Kurt Vonnegut: "I came to reading late, and I had wandered into the science fiction stacks at the library, mostly because of the illustrated covers, but the books themselves could be thick and dull, nothing at all like watching Star Trek on TV. I don't remember if someone recommended Vonnegut or if I'd just heard of him, but there he was with the other science fiction novels. In the middle of one of his books I'd be amazed at where he'd taken me. If I had to explain it to someone I would have failed, but it all made perfect sense in the moment. He achieved what I didn't know fiction could do. And while I haven't revisited his work, that's the feeling I'm always chasing."

"Not a fan of Vonnegut," Allison said, as if that were the final word on him. "Sorry."

"Maybe you had to be a boy in Indiana in the 1970s."

Goldman who had been eavesdropping while pretending to talk with Sparrow, left the conversation to walk past the group of writers, and he said, simply, "Cheever," without qualification or explanation, and he moved on to the next room where there was fruit and cheese.

Jeff Tequila said, "Hemingway," which was pretty common, he knew, but he added, "which is what led me to the Minimalist, and to Mississippi."

Trisha A. rolled her eyes at Hemingway, but she'd read him too, before she was enlightened, and she'd always liked his first book of stories, which was more experimental and she knew would still stand up had it been written today.

"Please don't say *Old Man and the Sea*," Maya added.

"No," the guy agreed. "But I like *Sun Also Rises* and *Moveable Feast*."

Maya said hers was, "Gabriel Garcia Marquez," but we all knew this about her. She had said so in workshops, in interviews, in each acknowledgements page to each of her books. If there was an opportunity to sidestep reality in one of her stories, she always took it. She also revealed repeatedly that she had had an imaginary friend when she was young, and that she believed we were in a hologram or a video game, or whatever metaphor might fit, Plato's cave if you will, and that our primary purpose was not to love, or to help each other, or to alleviate suffering, which were all as fleeting and impermanent as losing a Super Mario as another immediately took his place, but our purpose, our reason for being, and the experience we were most perfectly wired for, was to be entertained.

"The church of Disney?" Trent said.

"Not Disney per se," Maya said, "but if that's what you love, then yes."

"There's no sin, no wasting time, no bacchanal. It's not good or right or moral. It just is, and it's what we do, and what we should do. We should watch TV, go to sporting events, go to comedy clubs. And this war-weary save-the-children Sarah McLaughlin pet-shelter guilt is against our natures and it's bad for us."

"Guilt causes cancer?"

"Cancer causes cancer, and cancer is awful, but if it's *your* cancer don't rub it on my conscience. I'm sorry that you're sick but I'm not obligated to feel bad for you."

Trisha A.'s response to her own question was a calculated reply that was true enough but also not faithful to the spirit of the question. She said, "*Sweet Valley High*," and she let her admission sink in. She was a voracious reader when she was small and was reading the series when she was much too young for it, and while it didn't shape her or inform her future reading choices, it was formative in the way these books could both accept and reject feminism and do so in a way that was decidedly anti-literary. While she found Maya's flippant response to human suffering deplorable, she also understood that the *Madame Bovarys*, *Ivan Illychs*, and *Anna Karenninas* could be a huge drag for a reader. She still hadn't read Celine, or Hugo, or Zola, and she didn't intend to. She didn't read anything like *Sweet Valley High* anymore, but she had once enjoyed them greatly. *Sweet Valley High* taught her to stare at a culturally significant object that was ignored by the literary establishment and to find all kinds of interesting things to say about it. Much like she'd learned to do with

Pinterest, or Chipotle, or Nicki Minaj.

"I *loved* the twins," Maya said.

"The twins are the shit," Trisha agreed.

Since Goldman had walked away from her, Sparrow joined the group and she said, "*To Kill a Mockingbird.*"

"Really?" Allison said, surprised.

Even Scott had read that one and he nodded his approval.

"I mean I know it's popular all over again right now," Sparrow said. "I just loved it. I wanted to be..."

And Allison, and Maya, and Trent, and Trisha, all finished her sentence for her, "Scout."

"She was the coolest."

Trisha A. excused herself to find iMOL, who she spotted in the next room, they made eye contact, and she joined the group of lit. professors to spring her question on them, "Tell me, gents. Who ruined you? Which author made you head-over-heals for literature and dragged you down into some other century?"

Her question was answered without contemplation and with no hesitation as they each named off their scholarly specialties:

"Wallace Stevens."

"Wordsworth."

"Shakespeare, of course."

"After a brief dalliance with Homer I eventually found my way to my true love, John Milton."

"No, no, no," Trisha said. "Not who do you study, or who are you paid to talk about in classrooms. Who made you want to read? Who made you want to become literary experts?"

"The same."

"The same."

"The same."

"At first it was Homer. Then it was John Milton."

Trisha shook her head. "Surely, you were kids once. Surely, you've read for pleasure. Mine was *Sweet Valley High*."

"Oh dear."

"Let me guess, you were one of the creative writers here?"

"Kids don't read Homer. Kids don't read Wallace Stevens."

"Maybe it was Dickens first, I don't recall."

"It's just a question. I was curious. None of you read Superman comics or Mickey Spillane?"

"Oh heavens no. I do like a good 007 every now and again."

In the next room where there was disco music, and the furniture had been been pushed out into the hall but no one danced, Goldman hovered over the famous writer's girlfriend but no one heard what was being said. He asked urgent questions and she shook her head or shrugged her shoulders. He had wanted to know about the manuscript, but she hadn't read it, she didn't know what to say. Was it complete? Was it good? Why hadn't she sent it to him?

Goldman had to lean in close as she explained what Trent looked like and where he could be found. If he needed to know about the book, Trent could answer his questions. If he wanted to represent the book and try to sell it, he should give her some figures. What might it be worth? What should she expect?

Goldman wasn't prepared to make promises that might not pan out. He could sell a book that petered out, or a book that ranged somewhere between mediocre and poor, but he couldn't sell a terrible book, and so he needed to know more before he would give the girlfriend any estimate of royalties.

Goldman went back into the kitchen where Trent was last seen, and as he walked past the group of alumni he said, "The Swimmer," to add to his earlier one-word comment, "Cheever."

He checked the back porch, since he thought Trent might be a smoker, and there were smokers, of cigarettes and also of a jay that was being passed around, with some current students and Dr. Cleary, the linguist, all taking deep long hits. Goldman stepped in, took a long pull himself, and he coughed it back out as he went around to the front of the house, and back inside.

Because there was nowhere else to go, Goldman went up the stairs, and he found Trent in the famous writer's bedroom, standing in front of the closet mirror and looking at himself in a pair of the famous writer's shoes. He was taking pretend exaggerated steps and was suddenly embarrassed when he saw Goldman in the mirror, and Trent realized he'd been caught.

"There are holes."

"I beg your pardon?"

"In the shoes," Trent said, and he lifted a foot to show Goldman that the famous writer's shoes had been worn down and there was a hole in the middle of each of the soles.

"Is your plan to steal them?"

"I wanted to know what they felt like."

"Feels funny?"

"Feels funny."

"I was sent up here to ask about the book."

"What do you want to know?"

"Everything."

"I was advised to get a linguistic analysis."

"By her?"

"By someone else. Who thinks the book might not be his."

"Why are you telling me?"

"You don't care?"

"No one will care. No one will know. This girlfriend wouldn't dare come clean. It would be the end of her. You think it's hers?"

"Yes, but she doesn't want a writing career."

"Well good. She's not going to have one."

"I've also been advised that if we are going to work together on this, you should look at something of mine."

"By her."

"By me. Little voice in my head."

"Understandable," Goldman said. "But not necessary. I know who you are. I can't sell your work."

"*You* know who I am?"

"Sure. I used to sometimes ask if he could recommend any writers. Your name came up at one point. You're a good writer but I'm not in love with your work."

"They all say that."

"We all say it, or we all say it to you?"

"What's the difference?"

"Look, I'm sorry. I know it's disappointing."

"He recommended me to you?" Trent said. "When was this? Did he send you something or did you look at something online?"

"I don't remember. It doesn't matter. If you feel you can't work with me, I understand. Why don't you find an editor who would be good for your work, and that will be who we approach with this book of his. It gives you a reason to contact that editor, and when the time is right, after you've written a really great preface, you broach the subject of your own work with this editor."

"But you won't represent me, not even for the right editor?"

"No, I won't."

"An editor's not going to look at anything I send unless it comes through an agent."

"They might. Then again, you may be right. But consider this: if I'm the one sending out this last book of his, no one will question the authorship, and you can ask for a finder's fee or an editor's fee, or whatever. Let's say you get a flat fee for the preface but this editor also gives you one percent royalties?"

"I can ask for that?"

"That I support."

"I'll give you 1% if you at least try to sell one of my books."

"I can't do it, Trent. I say 'no' to very talented people all the time, sometimes for years. I'm not going to be persuaded. I have to say 'no' to maintain the Goldman touch. I wish you luck. I hope you prove me wrong. But I can only represent something that's going to last, and you don't have what it takes to last."

"What is that, anyway?"

"No one knows."

As Trent stood there he saw Holly Rorsch walk toward them, but when she saw Trent and Goldman in discussion, she backed away and went back down the stairs. Trent didn't know who she was, but instinct told him not to take Goldman's offer, not yet.

"I need to think some more," Trent said. "I'm not trying to play hard. I do understand where you're coming from. But I'm going to get that linguistic analysis. You may not care, but I need to know."

Trent followed Holly Rorsch, but it wasn't until he was halfway down the stairs that he remembered he was wearing the famous writer's shoes. Instead of going back into his room and facing Goldman again, Trent turned on the stairs and he tied each shoe, which was loose but fit well enough he could pull it off.

In the living room, Trisha A. and iMOL had taken over the stereo and they were in the center of a crowd of current students who jumped up-and-down in unison to electronic dance music that crescendoed and tremors threatened to topple a display cabinet of china, the remains of the famous writer's first and second marriages. Trent danced between them and into the dining room where the platter of cheeses was decimated and the literature professors had either left or moved on to other nooks of the party. Everyone who wasn't dancing was either in the kitchen or on the back porch. Maya Drake was in a tight embrace with the famous writer's girlfriend. She was saying her goodbyes. She moved toward Trent, who was between her and the backdoor, and she gave him a less meaningful hug.

"Why are you leaving so soon?" he said. "You've got nowhere to go."

"I still have to respond to everyone's stories."

"You haven't done that?"

"I've been meaning to."

"Do you have a favorite, just between you and me?"

"I liked them all about the same."

Trent didn't think Maya could be any more evasive. The stories were so unalike there was no way anyone could like them about the same. He suspected she hadn't read them yet, and given all the pages between tonight and tomorrow, she probably wouldn't.

Because Maya noticed everything Trent stuttered through his goodbye to her while she stared down at his shoes.

"Don't ask," was all he could muster.

"I get it," she said, and she turned and went out the door.

As soon as Maya was gone it bothered him. He felt there was work he was missing out on and that she would get ahead, even though he'd read and written his responses to each of the stories. He suspected she'd go to her dorm room, charged from what this unusual night had brought, and she'd crank out a new story or another essay, and he wanted to do that too, though he'd have no one to send anything to, and like everything else, if he wrote, the story or essay would ferment on his hard drive for years before it finally landed at some literary magazine, not one worth bragging about but difficult enough to get into that he alone would understand the accomplishment.

He saw Allison and Scott through the kitchen window, Scott with his arm around her, not in an intimate way but as if he were making a show of ownership. They were with Holly Rorsch and Jeff Tequila, and they passed a spliff around. Maya had stopped to say goodbye to them to, and Trent wanted to get in on the spliff but he had to wait until Maya left, because he'd already said goodbye to her and following her outside would be weird. He stared out the window and muttered to himself, "Leave Maya. Leave," but she and Allison effused a pretend familiarity for far too long and Scott was Bogarting the marijuana, so Trent went out there anyway, and he sidled up next to Scott who handed him the spliff.

Allison was in the middle of saying how much she *loved* the story Maya had sent out for the workshop, using the word 'loved' repeatedly and always with emphasis. Maya had grown accustomed to these kinds of compliments and she accepted the praise by nodding each time 'loved' punctuated Allison's flattery. But Allison, who was high from the spliff, and obviously not used to being high, couldn't hide her true feelings as her speech slowed and she eventually stopped talking mid-sentence because Maya had not returned the compliment. She hadn't said *anything* about Allison's story and it was clear that since she hadn't by this point, that she never would. A flat frown took over Allison's face as she realized Maya was going to criticize her story tomorrow, and she wracked her brain to try to guess what Maya hadn't liked about it, though she came up with nothing. She had always suspected that Maya was in possession of some great secret at the same time she believed Maya had managed to fool everyone and she was lucky enough that the exact right people happened to go along.

The weed was good, and Trent was joyously emotional as a wave of glad sadness washed over him. He nodded his appreciation to Jeff Tequila, who had obviously been the one to bring the stuff. He puffed on it a good long while, then he handed it back to Jeff before it had been smoked down to the nub, and Jeff took a last hit, let the roach fall to the ground and he stepped on it as he walked back into the house. Maya had also departed, which left Trent high and with Allison and her husband. He had never met Allison's husband, and he remembered that something had given him the impression that Allison had told her husband about Trent's advances at some point.

It was not cute the way Allison fished for compliments or the way she came undone after a couple of hits of pot, but she looked beautiful in her casual red cocktail dress, her toes painted to match, Allison barefoot, having abandoned the high heels she had shown up in that proved to be of little utility. The fact that Scott had handed Trent the joint helped to lessen his long-felt idea of Scott as his nemesis, even if it hadn't been nor ever would be Scott's weed. He had seen how awkwardly Scott had moved about the party, how he was unable to engage in any kind of conversation about literature, and how he tagged along behind Allison who had returned to her old school a relatively successful writer. As much as they were mismatched, Trent saw that Scott provided the money that she needed to live the way she did, something he'd never be able to do, and while she'd settled somewhat by marrying Scott, she would have settled even more to be with him. Scott was achingly ordinary and someone Trent would have no time for at any other social event, but here they were, thrust together by circumstance and sizing each other up.

"Have you got somewhere to be during the workshop?" Trent asked him.

"I've got some Netflix to catch up on," Scott said. "I don't mind a hotel room."

"Have you tried meditation?" Trent asked and Allison shot him a glare because it was such a Trent thing to ask. Of course her husband hadn't tried meditation, but maybe he would have since meditation wasn't only for certain kinds of people anymore, as Trent had implied.

"Like a Buddhist?" Scott said. "I'd get bored."

"That's the thing," Trent said. "You do it like twenty minutes and you're more at peace with yourself. You don't have to try to occupy yourself with stimulation, and you don't get bored."

"I don't need stimulation. I was just going to watch Netflix."

Allison quickly intervened by introducing Trent to Holly Rorsch, because nothing good was going to come from Scott and Trent talking. She said Holly's name slowly, to tip Trent off that she was someone he should know. And he did recognize her name. He had sent her a couple of his novels over the years and after nine months of sitting on them Holly Rorsch had finally rejected each, in turn, with the comment, "I'm just not in love with this."

Trent hated agents viscerally. When he got one of these rejections the bitterness would fester in him for days. There were agents who rejected with form letters that tried to buffer the rejection by saying the work was really well-written and the writer obviously talented, which infuriated him because it couldn't be true if they sent the same letter to everyone. There were agents who rejected with form letters that were poorly written, and it infuriated him because they must have sent the same thing out thousands of times without recognizing their own bad prose, so how could they possibly be in a position to judge anyone else's? There were agents who probably thought they were being more genuine by not using a form rejection, except they used the same phrases over and over that all of them used, and Holly was one of these, who had told him she was "not in love with" his book, which was bizarre because it sounded like breaking up with someone you never dated in the first place, and this was exactly what Trent hated about online dating sites that required women to perform the same dance of rejection before they'd even met 90% of the guys, though the dating sites were also worth it because he'd met his current girlfriend online and he hoped to also one day land a literary agent.

While Holly had no memory of ever rejecting Trent's books, she knew who he was, and she lit up, because she understood that Trent was in possession of the famous writer's last novel. He was the only one here who had read it. In fact, he was the only person who had read it other than the famous writer, who was now dead. So Trent had something Holly desperately wanted and because he hated agents, his understanding of the situation, as well as his first dose of THC in a while, provided him with delicious glee. When she asked, he was fully prepared to say he "wasn't in love" with the dead writer's book, though he didn't do that, which was the right choice, since Holly was the only agent who'd ever been interested in him, even if it had nothing to do with his own work.

He chose his words carefully, "I think readers will be surprised. There's a contemporariness we haven't seen in his work, which was mostly Modern in style. He's not afraid to curlicue his sentences here."

"Art for art's sake?" Holly said. "I love it!"

"I don't think it will be widely loved."

"Oh?" Holly said. "He's always been a writer's writer. Nothing wrong with that."

"In this one he's less of a writer's writer."

"That can be good too," Holly said. "I'd love to be the one to sell it," which was probably too forward and no one said anything after that, the idea left to linger. So she added, "Not for the money, of course, but to be involved with it. With him."

Allison had been hanging on Trent's every word, reminded that not only was Maya going to shit on her story but the famous writer's girlfriend had rejected her too. Trent was talented in his own way but how could she, a woman even, have picked his story over hers?

"We'll never know what he might have written next," Allison said, something sure to be repeated by anyone who spoke at his service tomorrow, but everyone agreed with her since it was the polite thing to do.

And Holly Rorsch let on that she'd seen Trent and Goldman in the famous writer's bedroom together, and she said, only half-joking, "Did you catch Goldman snooping around looking for it," and she added, "someone should go up there. Goldman shouldn't be left alone in this house. Am I right?"

The mention of Goldman made Allison feel even lower. She

hadn't had a chance to talk to him, she'd been too scared, and now she was too high—there was no way. This had been her one chance, since at the memorial, well, it wouldn't seem right, though probably Goldman was used to it. Trent had known Allison a long time and he could tell she was unhappy. Scott was oblivious to her change in mood, and because of that she was also unhappy with him, which Trent loved, and he suspected her life's compromise of marrying him came with many moments like this.

"Holly's right," Trent said. "Someone should check on Goldman."

Scott smiled at Allison because it seemed all he'd heard about on this trip was how much she wanted to bump into him, and here was her chance, but she did not smile back, and what he'd failed to understand was that she'd given up on her fantasy of being represented by Goldman.

"Let's go inside," Scott said to Allison in the same poorly-acted nonchalance Trent suspected Scott used when he wanted sex. At any rate, Scott managed to pry Allison away before Trent and Allison had spent too much time with each other, and while Trent recognized the warm ashes of the long-nurtured crush he'd had on her, meeting Scott was something of a turn off because he reminded Trent of her less-likable and all-too predictable side. And while he felt Allison too had recognized the return of the vestigial crush she'd had on Trent, the one she'd snuffed out in its infancy and denied ever existed, unfortunately her stick of a husband was with her. And this woman, Holly, was suddenly intent on keeping Trent's attention, and he found that he was attracted to her. Holly had bright blue eyes behind stylish expensive blue-rimmed glasses and her light brown hair was cut in straight high bangs that made her forehead look large. He suspected the nature of her job in publishing meant her hair had to be tamed all of the time and she was on the chubby side though she wore it well, or as Trent would have said, "in all the right places," and he suspected she always wore black in order to encourage that impression.

"Now that we're alone," Holly said, "I want you to tell me everything about it."

The thing Trent dreaded the most about coming to this party was that he didn't want to have to talk to anyone about the book, which they would all read when it came out, and he didn't want to make judgments for them. He knew they all wanted him to say it was genius, but it wasn't, and even if the famous writer really was a genius, as Trent suspected he was, this book was not. But he moved his opinion slightly more in that direction for Holly's sake. If he could only come up with a suave way of suggesting the transaction, he got the impression that Holly would have sex with him tonight if he'd let her look at the book, and he would be up for that, and they'd both get what they wanted, which made it ethical, even if probably under almost no other circumstance would she ever consider going to bed with him, yet he was the one in a relationship, and his lack of imagination with respect to a good pick-up line also saved him from the guilt of cheating on the best girlfriend he'd had in decades. Trent was a good guy, mostly because he was honest and didn't know any other way to be. Serving art brought it out in him. Yes, he was also an asshole sometimes, but he tended to keep his asshole side under wraps until confronted with fakery.

Instead he and Holly talked about the Mars lander and the distance between planets, the near-perfect season of a baseball team she loved who were sure to crash in the playoffs, and the strange way Hollywood accidentally created a national fascination with writers by making films out of more and more books. And Holly said, "I practice meditation too, and I loved what you said, how it makes you no longer sick of yourself."

"I didn't quite use those words," Trent said.

"But that was your meaning."

And Trent, who had only minutes ago fantasized that he could somehow steal Allison from Scott, was suddenly enamored with Holly and though he had sworn not to give anyone a copy of the book, he could get her alone and read it to her, some of his favorite passages. And she would smile, and he would fall into her eyes, and she might only be doing it for the book, but he might forget his girlfriend back home for a night, with this literary agent who had summarily rejected him, more than once, and who would again if it weren't for the famous writer's last book.

The famous writer's girlfriend was in the bedroom of the famous writer and she walked out onto the small balcony, waved at Trent, and threw his shoes down.

"You left these up here!" she said.

"I meant to..." he said, but she went back inside and he saw she was talking with Goldman.

Holly looked up at them too.

"If you want this book," Trent said, "maybe you could represent one of mine."

"Goldman turned you down?"

"Of course he did."

"What do you have that I can sell?"

"Science fiction satire?"

"No."

"Literary satire?"

"No."

"Short stories?"

"Any that were in the *New Yorker?*"

"No."

"*Paris Review?*"

"No."

"No."

"Metafiction?"

"No."

"Post-Feminism?"

"Are you gay?"

"No."

"No."

"Ethnic memoir?"

"What ethnicity?"

"Italian-American."

"Mafia?"

"No."

"No."

"Post-apocalyptic dystopia?"

"For teens?"

"No."

"No."

"Magic-Realism?"

"Set in Africa or China?"

"No."

"No."

"What *can* you sell?"

"Books where villains change their identities to draw victims in."

"I don't have any villains."

"Books where survivors rebuild their lives and forgive their transgressors."

"I don't have books about survivors."

"Books where little kids visit heaven."

"All my kids are minor characters."

"Something Taylor Swift might be able to star in."

"No."

"A mom who solves the murder of her daughter after the police have given up?"

"No."

"Books for fifth graders with either a Star Wars or Minecraft tie-in?"

"No."

"Books for fifth graders where the girl becomes a C.E.O?"

"No."

"Is it really that bad?"

"Why do you write?"

"I'm good at it. I love doing it. I want to be read."

"The average American might read one or two books per year, which really means a small number read ten or more books while nearly everyone else never reads anything at all. And all those people who don't read, they might still buy a book, and when they do, they want something familiar. They don't want to be challenged. They don't want *weird*."

"You can't help me?"

"Send me your best book. I'll look at it."

"That's it?"

"What do you want from me? Even if I agree to represent a book I have to send it to editors with bosses who want blockbusters. Anyone who publishes you, even your very best book, is taking a loss."

"Except that it's a good book."

"A good book is one that sells. For people who don't read, they need to know that much about a book before it even has a chance of reaching them."

"Which has nothing to do with being good."

"Not in the way you and I understand it."

"Why do you do it?"

"I'm trying to find the rare writer who can do both."

"And then you can retire?"

"Not entirely but going about it more the way Goldman does. A lot more payback for a lot less work."

"Basically, I'm fucked?"

"You're lucky. You've got two out of three: you're good at it, and you love it. That's more than a lot of writers can say. After all, no one is making you write."

"True. I'm not one of those suffering writers."

"Except that that's something I may well be able to sell, depending on the source and magnitude of the suffering."

"Broke doesn't cut it, I'm guessing?"

"No. If you have all of your arms and legs and a brain that allows you to be nice to people you aren't truly suffering."

"There has to be something seriously wrong with me?"

"I'm rooting for you," Holly said. "I really am. But we don't live in a literary culture. Good writing is never going to be enough."

§

Back inside, Goldman walked past Allison and Scott, and Scott introduced himself because he wanted to help Allison, but Goldman misunderstood Scott. He thought Scott was the writer. Goldman was kind and upbeat as he left the party, but when he shook Scott's hand he also said, "I'm closed to submissions for the foreseeable future," and Goldman was gone.

This was good for Allison to hear. She already had a literary agent and getting over her fantasy of Goldman taking her on would allow her to be in the moment and enjoy the fellowship of the writers around her.

Trisha A. and iMOL had left, and the electronic dance music left with them, with the living room blaring one of the famous writer's Ray Charles CDs, and the thinned cadre of students didn't dance but swayed and sang along in a drunk reverie. The famous writer's girlfriend had gone upstairs to bed, as the famous writer often had when he'd thrown parties, leaving the front door unlocked and trusting that eventually everyone would go.

There were bookshelves of signed first editions from the other Minimalists and each of the writers he'd invited to Petal for readings. In the hallway hung three framed certificates of his teaching awards. Near the decimated plate of cheeses was an untouched corked decanter of Scotch that was assumed to be too expensive to drink, except that it was Dewar's and had been left out for the party. Trent's shoes were in the yard where they'd landed. Cigarette butts were under bushes and a snuffed-out roach lay in the middle of the back porch. One of the students had been kind enough to carry out a bag of trash. The TV was still on with the sound down, the basketball game over, the local news over, Saturday Night Live over, with the rest of the A.M. left to reruns of cop shows and infomercials. There were half-filled plastic cups spread around the rooms, three on an end table, two on the fire place mantle, seven on the island in the kitchen, one on a window sill outside. The moon was covered by a cloud. A police siren was heard in the distance.

The future of the Deep South Writers Program was in doubt. The patriarch was dead and the institution he had served didn't know what was best for itself. Another essay about the famous writer posted online, this one by a former student Lydia hadn't come across in her search and so this former student knew nothing about the reunion party, the memorial service, or the workshop. There were children who grew up with shitty parents and they never got over it. There were artists who were metaphorical children who only wanted to please metaphorical parents, and when one of them died it was unimaginable but also liberating. Who had they been writing for all those years? Even if the mentor saw the work and complimented the writer with a short congratulatory email, the critical voice was firmly implanted in their heads. It would never be okay to write something good that wasn't great. Without connections, without pedigree, without genius, there was only hard work and luck, never one or the other, because it had to be hard work *and* luck, both necessary, the work slow and steady, the luck immediate and unpredictable, unsummonable. The famous writer had gotten lucky when he was young by being associated with a literary trend. And he spent his time as a teacher making sure that all those young writers understood that this rare occurrence would most likely miss them. They were fools and idiots, just as he had been, stubborn in their faith in art, and bound to be disappointed if they continued down that path. This essay that had posted from the former student, the one Lydia hadn't found, gave the writers who read it the motive behind the famous writer's cutting criticism, and the brutally honest assessment of their futures. There would never be a world without art, but there would never be a world where anyone who wanted to make art should expect to be able to do so.

3

Lydia had been the liaison between the funeral director and the writers, who would have preferred to call him 'undertaker,' and they were disappointed when he didn't make an appearance at the funeral home. If Trent had written the story this undertaker would have been tall, in black tails and a top hat. iMOL would have added a monocle. Trisha A. would have given him a submissive wife who never spoke but flitted about to keep the procession of funerals on time. As each came into the funeral home their writer's sensibilities were on alert. They knew there was a high probability of writing a funeral scene one day, and the details of the establishment and the sights and sounds of the place were being recorded in memory. They also knew that Maya had already published an essay about the dead writer in *Atlantic Online* so there was interest, and this get-together was very likely a good angle to pursue.

As each arrived they felt the palpable anxiety in anticipation of having a story workshopped, and it was coming from everyone. It was an old feeling, one they hadn't experienced in years, but here it was again, like a dreadful friend. Each had the confidence of know-ing they possessed a particular skill that was valued by these other writers who would see what was best about their writing and com-mend it. But these writers were also very picky readers, having devoted themselves to the vocation religiously. They would recognize any shortcuts, any clichés, any weak points in the fictive dream. As writers they wanted to be understood and loved. As readers they wanted to be transported and wowed. The likelihood of these things happening, especially since each story would not only be seen in relation to the other stories workshopped, but in relation to all of literature, was not very good. These writers, who had a deep affection for each other and each other's writing, had worked very hard to achieve certain failure.

The sign in the lobby directed them to the dead writer's closed visitation, with a public visitation at 2:30 PM and a service and burial to follow at 3:30 PM. The room was as they'd requested, with folding chairs in addition to the pews, so they could arrange themselves in a circle. The best way to do this, as Trent and iMOL assessed the layout of the small chapel, was to move the nickel casket that held the dead writer to make space for their circle, which was more like an oval. And since it seemed disrespectful to put the dead writer's closed casket on the side of the room, they placed him on the ground in the middle of the circle of chairs.

As the writers arrived, each acknowledged their dead mentor on the floor by placing a palm on the casket and praying, or quieting the mind, or trying to convey thoughts to the old atheist across the divide. Then each took a seat in the circle, and they clutched their written responses, printed out stories, and notes, with pens at the ready. They had until 2:30 PM to battle with each other in the service of literature, with bathroom breaks, with snacks in the small kitchen that separated this small chapel from the adjacent one, with a service that would soon commence in the neighboring chapel, of a beloved grandma and they would need to keep their voices down no matter how heated it got, because they didn't have permission to do what they were doing. They were supposed to be spending time with the body and chatting with each other in soft sentences. If the undertaker made a surprise appearance, they agreed to immediately act as if they were conducting a prayer circle. They suspected that the way they'd arranged the chairs around him would freak the undertaker out enough that he'd certainly leave them alone again.

iMOL proposed that they workshop in the order that the manuscripts had been received, that way they'd start with the ones they'd had the most time to think about, which advantaged him because he was the second to send out his story. It meant going right after Maya, who had sent her story out first and was a tough act to follow, but he'd get it over with relatively quickly and wouldn't have to sit and fester as the hours wore on. Everyone but Maya agreed, which meant there was something from someone's story she wanted to talk about right away.

So iMOL volunteered, "I can go first if you want."

"It's not that," Maya said. "I don't mind going first."

"Then let's begin," iMOL said. "Did everyone read Maya's story? Should we start with a summary and a favorite passage?"

"Don't I get to say something?" Maya asked.

"Yes, of course. Go ahead."

"I don't know what to say. I hope you liked it."

And they agreed that they liked it, though they would soon level the critical gaze at this poor story that was bound to take some hits for its simplicity and the ease for which it slipped out of realism and into an enchanted fantasy where babies in high chairs formed words in their alphabet cereal and infirm old folks in dining halls formed words in their alphabet soup.

Allison volunteered to summarize, of course. She risked trashing the story from the outset, but since everyone knew Allison was extremely jealous of Maya the discussion proceeded with as much objective fairness as one could level at a story where babies could spell and old folks were served alphabet soup at every meal.

"What bothered me," Allison said, "was the way the story put so much emphasis on the words that were formed, that it felt forced. It had me disbelieving."

"We should get some examples," Trent said.

"One word is 'trust.' Another is 'Enbrel'."

"I didn't know that one. I had to look it up."

"It's an arthritis medication."

"So there were words charged with positive connotations and words that were more pedestrian. I couldn't make out why this was happening or why I was supposed to care? Anybody else?"

Trisha A. said, "I went along with it. While the pedestrian words may not have meant much to us, they did for those people. Each was a slice of the psyche of the character as they showed up and then exited the story."

Maya, who was not allowed to talk while they discussed her story nodded profusely in agreement with Trisha, but the other workshop participants tried to ignore her and to carry on.

"I could have used a little more consistency," Allison said. "I mean letters might float on the surface of soup but getting them to line up would take more than a spoon."

"*I* could do it with a spoon."

"But these characters are *old*. And babies can't spell."

"You already said that. There's magic here and this is how magic would manifest if it were ever to return to our world."

Maya was beaming, pleased to find an ally in Trisha A.

Trisha A. added, "I was a little disappointed in the sexism."

This got everyone leafing back through the pages of the story to look for whatever it was she might be referring to.

"Please explain."

"These babies are wearing pink and blue, and they're playing with Barbies for goddess' sake. I wanted them to have more progressive families. It just gave me the feeling that their talents would be wasted because their parents were pigs."

"It's kind of an archetype," Trent said. "If you look at the Bible stories and the stories of the saints. I mean look at Jesus. The special ones are always coming from ordinary families. The magi, the seers, the Einsteins—they don't come from royalty. The aristocrats are going out of their way to dress in jewels and to sit in the front pew of the church. So I don't think it's sexist at all. It's just how ordinary people are. They dress girls in pink and they buy them Barbie dolls."

"But I don't want them to be ordinary. Maybe we could have one character with enlightened parents who was raised gender-neutral. That way the reader could see that the writer doesn't actually condone gender binaries."

"That's not what the story's about."

"But it's in there."

"Was anyone else distracted by having characters named Molly and Emilia?"

"I was able to tell them apart, so it didn't bother me."

"I was too, but they sounded too much alike."

"Good point. Easy enough to fix. It's been noted. The writer can choose to make the change if she wants. We seem to support giving them more distinct names."

"Does anyone care if I bring that box of donuts in here?"

"I don't know if we're allowed to eat in here."

"I'm a very meticulous eater. I won't make a mess."

"I'd like a donut."

"No, I mean because of the dead body. Is there some kind of OSHA code?"

"It does seem kind of taboo."

"We put him on the floor. That was probably taboo too."

"What do you think he would say?"

"He wouldn't care if we ate, as long as it was something he liked as well."

"No, I mean about Maya's story."

"It's Maya's. He'd fucking love it. She could shit words and he'd tell us we needed to write more like her."

Which prompted Maya to break protocol and speak, "I resent that. It's not my fault he liked my writing more than yours. And I would also like a donut."

"I'm going to go get them. Anyone grossed out by this, this is your last chance to speak."

The box was passed around but was paused when iMOL couldn't decide which one he wanted.

"Are you going to touch them all?" Allison said, which made him blush, but she was right, no one was talking about the story anymore and they were all watching him pick at the donuts.

"Save me a cinnamon twist."

"There's two cinnamon twists. I'm sure one will make it to you."

"The lemon-filled is really good."

"Any other comments about Maya's story?"

"We haven't talked about the ending."

"Yes, we should."

"I liked the ending."

"I expected something more."

"Like what?"

"It was good. I just wanted more."

"Like how?"

"You know. More."

"I know what she means."

"Can you articulate it?"

"We learn that there's this untapped human potential. So I'm waiting for this big reveal, or a metaphor that just ties it all together. An epiphany."

"I *love* an epiphany."

"What kind of epiphany would we get here?"

"I don't agree. I mean Maya has never written an epiphany. She's never going to. It's not what she does. She puts some magic in, it's relatively entertaining, and then it ends flat. It's worked pretty well for her so far."

"Ouch."

"I'm only saying what Colonel Kurtz would have unleashed on any of us, but for her he never did."

"Why is that, I wonder?"

"Three words: low, cut, blouse."

"She did bring out the cleavage for workshop today."

"I can't believe this, you guys. It's so fucking sexist. Maya can dress any way she pleases. She can sell her body if she wants. She can manipulate the male gaze. It's her cleavage and its very nice cleavage and I support her right to display boobage whenever and however."

"I'm sitting right here, you guys."

"Yeah, that's unfair. We need to direct the conversation back to the story. We're fifty-fifty on the ending, some of us like it, some of us want more, which I'm interpreting as something more in tune with a traditional story ending. For myself, I prefer to see a writer subvert the norm, so I'm not in favor of the traditional ending, even if this is mostly a traditional story."

"That's the thing. We've seen this a thousand times, so it creates an expectation. And it's not like avoiding a traditional ending is doing anything experimental, it's only flat and unsatisfying because the expectation was created with no follow-through. Me? I'd gut the expectation. I'd go non-traditional the whole way."

"How does one do that?"

"That's for the writer to figure out."

"Okay, Maya. I think we're winding down. Anything else you want to say?"

"Thank you for your comments. I'll take them under consideration."

"That's it?"

"That's all she ever says."

"I'm just not going to change the story, okay? I like it how it is. *Antioch Review* has already accepted it."

"Wow! Congratulations."

"I'd still fix the ending."

"Let's move on. Anybody need a break?"

"Am I up?" iMOL said and there was a silence that didn't feel like agreement.

Maya spoke up, "There's something I have to say about Trent's story and I don't want to sit here any longer. I have to say it."

"I guess we're doing Trent's story next. Even though it went out late."

"His always go out late."

"I was making last minute changes."

"Really?" Maya said. "You expect us to believe that?"

"Spit it out."

"This story didn't read like one of Trent's," Maya said.

"You're saying I plagiarized a story?"

"Yes, I suspected this. So I gave a copy to Dr. Cleary along with copies of some of your other stories. He did a linguistic analysis and said there is no way you wrote this story."

"A linguistic analysis? What other stories did you send? Stuff from fifteen years ago?"

"These were recent. I Googled you and found some stuff you published online."

"So the only time you actually seek out my writing is to discredit it?"

"I think if we are going to workshop this story, we need to discuss the possibility that it may not actually be yours."

"Okay."

"Okay what?"

"It's his," Trent said and he nodded toward the coffin. "I put my name on it but it's his."

"Whose?"

"Him right there." He pointed.

"Why would you do that?"

"I wanted to know what people really thought. You're going to read his book when it comes out and everyone will be all gaga over it, but I wondered what you'd really think about the writing, about the book itself, if you were able to read it without associating it with him."

"Well, now we can't."

"You can thank Maya."

"I was just trying to keep the workshop honest."

"So you critiqued all our stories, which we worked our asses off on, but you didn't even write one?"

"I wrote one. That's why it came in late. I had every intention of workshopping my story, but then Maya said maybe his book was really written by his girlfriend and so it gave me the idea. I'd read the book and liked it well enough but had no idea what to really think, since there was all this other baggage with it."

"You were expecting us to help you with your preface?"

"I just wanted some feedback."

"Well, I thought it sucked. Can I say that?"

The comment provoked silence in its directness, and in the silence a distinct *thunk* was heard.

"Sucked how?"

"Are we workshopping this story? Are we really going to trash him with his dead body right there?"

"I think so. Why not? We ate the donuts."

"It sucked because I didn't give a shit about these people's problems. They live these pampered lives. I don't even know if any of them work. And then they're fucking each other, and so they don't have real problems but go out of their way to create problems for themselves that otherwise wouldn't exist."

"I think sexual attraction is something people give in to. And so in that respect it's not always 100% in their control."

"Some people court sexual attraction with cleavage."

"Are we still talking about Maya's boobs? Can we please move on?"

And there was another *thunk*. This time it was undeniable, and when it happened the casket moved.

"Did you see that?"

"No."

"Me neither."

"So you thought it sucked because people without jobs were fucking each other?"

"I mean hasn't that been done to death? Are we still interested in that?"

"Ask Lena Dunham."

"Are you talking about *Girls*? They have jobs."

"An internship is not a job."

"I like *Girls*."

"Me too."

"It's okay. There's a difference between watching fucking and reading about it, though."

"So you think his story should be a movie?"

"Absolutely not. I was bored to death."

"You don't think it would be more interesting as a movie, since there'd be naked people in it?"

"Naked people can be boring too."

"True."

The *thunk* was heard again and there was no denying that it came from the casket, which moved enough that its orientation shifted twenty or thirty degrees.

"Look at this: we're trashing him and he's rolling over in his grave."

"He's not in his grave."

"You know what I mean. He's rolling over. Watch: his writing sucks balls. I don't know how he was ever our teacher when he was such a shitty writer."

And the body rolled in the casket and the casket moved.

"Is he alive in there?"

"Can't be. He's been dead a long time."

"In Victorian times they buried people who were unconscious. In comas. That's how the vampire myth started."

"We should let him out."

"Really? You think we should we let him out?"

It was muffled, but from inside the casket a voice was heard, and he said, "Let me out!"

"How do we let him out? Do we need a key? Do we get the undertaker?"

"We *do not* get the undertaker."

"Go look in the kitchen. See if there's a knife or something. We can pry it open."

And he was heard inside the casket, and he said, "Pry it open!"

Trent and iMOL went over to the kitchen and they came back with cake knives they used to unlatch the lid, and the top half of the nickel casket swung open. There was an aroma that rushed out and made a sickly tingle in the sinuses, formaldehyde and something sweet. He was drained of blood and embalmed. He was definitely not alive, but he sat up. His skull was crushed on one side with his face stitched into a wad that was never meant to be seen. He was held together but severely deformed.

He gurgled words but his jaw was also sewn shut.

"Give me that!" he mumbled and he took the knife from Trent, which he moved around in his mouth until he was able to free his jaw, and he spoke clearly, as clearly as he could with his bent and confused face. "What the hell are you doing workshopping my shit?"

"It was Trent's idea."

The dead writer still held the knife, which he pointed at them when he talked, but Trent wasn't afraid. As abusive as his mentor had sometimes been, he never would have stabbed anyone.

"Who gave you my book?"

"It's really yours?"

"Of course it's mine."

"When the linguist told me he was 100% sure this story wasn't Trent's, I asked if he thought it was yours, and while he said there were some phrases that were found elsewhere in your work, the verbal patterns varied enough that he put it at fifty-fifty."

"Fifty-fifty? Are you fucking kidding me? Who is this guy?"

"Dr. Cleary. I also showed him samples from your girlfriend's writing and he put her at fifty-fifty too. Are we looking at some kind of collaboration?"

"Cleary's an ass. You know that guy tells everyone he's a vegetarian but he eats chicken."

"It's probably easier to say 'vegetarian' than to try to explain 'vegetarian plus chicken.'"

"He eats chicken all the time. Since when is chicken a vegetable?"

"Was the book a collaboration?"

"Maybe."

"What do you mean, maybe? Either it is or it isn't."

"That is so sexist. You were going to publish it without giving her credit?"

"I wasn't going to publish it. Not yet anyways. I was saving it."

"For what?"

"For this, I guess."

"Tell us Lazarus, what you've seen."

"Very funny."

"He got the allusion. I didn't think he'd get it. He was always talking about movies."

"I've read the Russians. That's a great story. Why wouldn't I know it?"

"Should we call her up? Shouldn't she be here if she contributed?"

"You can't let her see me like this."

"You're the one who crawled back out."

"I'm stuck in here. Help me sit up."

He reached around in the casket to find objects in there with him, which he grabbed and tossed out, paperback copies of his books.

"What the hell is this shit?"

"I believe they're called 'effects'."

"You thought I wanted to be buried with books? Like I'm going to bide my time in eternity with reading. Is there even a reading light in here?"

"They're *your* books. Your life's work."

"I'm through with books. I've been through with books for a while."

"But you were our mentor."

"It was a job. What else was I going to do?"

"Have you noticed Maya's cleavage?"

"Maya's here?"

He twisted around until he saw her and she gave him an embarrassed wave.

"She's the one who gave you away. We'd have thought this was Trent's story."

"Trent who?"

"Oh great. He doesn't even remember me."

"Oh him. What are we all doing here exactly?"

"This is a workshop."

"I know that. But why?"

"Why not?" Trent said.

"Why not, indeed."

"We were planning a reunion, but then you died."

"What does that have to do with this?"

"We thought it would be fun."

"Is anyone having fun?"

"No one is having fun."

"Maybe 'fun' isn't the right word. It's how we knew each other. It seemed it might be natural. We'd get feedback."

"Isn't feedback overrated?"

"That's not what you used to tell us."

"You signed up for it. But that's over. You don't have to do this."

"We wanted to."

"Why?"

"Are we going to workshop this story or not?"

"Excerpt. We know now that it's not a story, but an excerpt. I would have liked to have known that going in."

"You don't think it can stand alone?" Trent said. "I tried to pick an excerpt that could work as a story."

"Why did he have my book?"

"Your girlfriend gave it to him."

"Are you fucking my girlfriend?"

"No. Why is everything about fucking with you?"

"Not everything."

"It was hers to give, not only as your heir, but as co-author."

"Why would she give it to him?"

"We've also been trying to figure that out."

"She asked us for writing samples and she liked my story best."

"Which none of us has seen because he handed in your story instead."

"Excerpt."

"He handed in your excerpt instead."

"I thought it was great."

"You're only saying that because he's in the room with us. Five minutes ago you thought it was mine and you were ready to trash me. Admit it. What does it say in your notes? Be honest."

"One note, and this isn't necessarily a criticism, but one note that I have is that the sex scenes weren't very sexy."

"They're not supposed to be sexy."

"You're not allowed to talk. You can say something before we workshop and at the end when we're done, but while we critique your story you have to remain quiet."

"Can I say something to start off?"

"Go ahead."

"The sex scenes aren't supposed to be sexy."

"Is that it?"

"If I think of something else, I'll say it."

"No, it doesn't work that way. You can say something now but then you have to be quiet."

"As if you're dead."

"As if your jaw is sewn shut."

"That's not funny."

"It's kind of funny."

"Okay, it's kind of funny."

"Anything else?"

"I'm done."

"Let's pick back up. We've got an opinion that the sex scenes are not sexy and are possibly not supposed to be sexy."

"Not 'possibly'. I told you they weren't."

"He's talking again."

"We have to remember that author intention does not necessarily translate into the reader experiencing everything the author wants. We can only tell you what we experienced as we read it, and it's up to you to decide how to go about fixing it."

"I'd fix it by making the sex scenes sexy."

"With cleavage."

"Can we please drop it?"

"You don't think cleavage is sexy? I think cleavage is hella sexy."

"I don't know. Cleavage has been done."

"Of course it's been done. If it works why change it?"

"It *does* work," the dead writer admitted.

"My problem is different. Before I can think that a person is sexy, I have to like them as a person. The character isn't on the page for me yet and all of a sudden we're hopping into bed."

"The character isn't sleeping with *you*. She's sleeping with Robert."

"I don't know very much about Robert *or* Samantha."

"But *they* know each other and we're going to get to know them over the course of the book."

"Excerpt."

"So maybe that's one thing that doesn't work as well as a story, but you can still want to know more about a character while you also know enough that it works."

"I'm saying it doesn't work. I don't know them. I don't know why they're attracted to each other. And I don't want to be in the room with them while they're doing it."

"Do people still say 'doing it'?"

"I do."

"You would."

"What is that supposed to mean?"

"I think you know what it means."

"The point, and it's a fair one, is that there may be an issue with believability and/or character depth. For some of us, sex aside, the characters may not be developed enough."

"These two characters are pretty much him and his girlfriend. Isn't that obvious?"

"But how can you cheat on your girlfriend, with your girlfriend?"

"The other one's his girlfriend. This one is, I don't know who."

"They both seem kind of like his girlfriend."

"I don't think he was getting out very much there at the end."

"Neither was she."

"Is she going to sell his house?"

"I would."

"Where does the house come up in the story? Did I miss it?"

"I meant the real girlfriend. His real house. She could sell it and move somewhere cool."

"You don't think Petal's cool?"

"No one thinks Petal is cool. Not even him."

"Okay, so now he's quiet."

"Probably sad about his house."

"Wouldn't you be?"

"I don't know. It's a house. We cross the River Styx alone. You can't take a house with you."

"Maybe he's sad about her leaving him."

"*He* left *her*. The house is irrelevant."

"It's relevant."

"There is no house in this story."

"Excerpt."

"There is no house. We shouldn't be talking about it."

"Can I just say that now that I know it's his excerpt there are all kinds of his own rules that he violated."

"Such as?"

"We have several characters without character descriptions."

"That's true."

"I noticed that."

"It's easy enough to fix. The writer should consider character descriptions when each new character is introduced."

"Isn't that formulaic?"

"A little, but it's forgivable."

"How is he going to fix it? He's dead."

"Someone should tell his girlfriend. She can fix it. What else?"

"I'm not going to be the one to tell her."

"Me neither."

"It's not important. What else?"

"He's got plot points coming through dialogue."

"Was that against one of his rules?"

"Yes. Especially major plot points."

"What should he do?"

"Cut those lines and put the plot points in the exposition."

"He's got whole sections without any exposition."

"I thought he hated Hemingway."

"He *loved* Hemingway. *You* hated Hemingway."

"He was a Minimalist. How could he hate Hemingway?"

"This didn't feel like Minimalism."

"I was worried about that."

"Why were you worried? Because people might say it's not really him?"

"It's not."

"It's half him."

"We don't know what percentage is him."

"I'd guess half."

"I'd say a third."

"I'm thinking more like two thirds."

"None of this is relevant. We need to keep it to the story. Or excerpt."

"The tag lines. At one point he actual used 'ululated'."

"He did not."

"I remember that. What page was that?"

"Noted. He can do a word find to locate it. It definitely stood out to me."

"And the adverbs."

"I also noticed the adverbs."

"See, that to me made me think it wasn't Minimalism. Name one Minimalist who uses adverbs."

"Can I just say I love Microsoft Word? I love it. The Word find. Find and replace. The squiggly green grammar-check lines. All of it."

"How can you love Microsoft anything?"

"Word works. Word is the best."

"I thought Google Docs was the thing now."

"It's okay. Kind of clunky. Word is definitely better. But who can afford it, am I right?"

"It's not that bad."

"More than I'd have to pay for a typewriter."

"True."

"But you need it. You could never get by on just a typewriter anymore."

"You can pirate Word on the torrents."

"Isn't that illegal? Won't they catch you?"

"I mean if pirating bothers you, then go ahead and pay for it. They haven't caught me."

"I didn't think of that. I thought the torrents was like for Metallica albums, Prince bootlegs, and low-def movies."

"There's that too. TV shows. A shit-ton of books."

"You *do not* pirate books."

"Sure I do."

"But you're a writer."

"It's all best sellers. Nothing any good. They don't need my money."

"Then why do you download it?"

"Just to have them. I might read one of them one day."

"You will not."

"Probably not."

"Did you pirate his books?"

"Bobby Knight? Absolutely."

"You read those, right?"

"I read a couple."

"He's doing really well keeping quiet."

"I can hear you."

"Is there more to say about this excerpt?"

"I think Trent needs to provide more context. So we understand how this excerpt fits in with the rest of the book. Is this from the beginning or from the middle somewhere?"

"It's not the beginning but pretty close. I thought it did a pretty good job of giving the reader a sense of the book as a whole."

"What else happens?"

"More of the same. And his mother dies or something."

"Or something?"

"It's kind of vague."

"How can that be vague? 'Mother' and 'dies' are extremely specific."

"I had to read it quickly."

"You're not sure if his mother died or not?"

"I think she dies."

"That's the big reveal? It's supposed to explain why he acts this way?"

"It's not a reveal. It's just something that happens."

"That you *think* happens."

"I'm pretty sure it happens, but it's kind of a side story."

"Flat characters fucking each other and his mother dies. Is that it?"

"That's pretty much it."

"Seems a little unfair."

"People are going to *love* this book."

"Did you love it?"

"I did not love it. But it wasn't marketed to me as the recently discovered masterpiece of one of our late greats."

"You don't think people can see past that?"

"Not any who will have their opinion published."

"With no one allowed to dismantle the façade?"

"Is there anything else? Any last thoughts?"

"I liked the sex scenes."

"You did not."

"I did."

"Why didn't you say anything?"

"I'm saying it now. Sex doesn't have to be sexy. Sex is mostly not sexy. So I appreciated that. I agree with him that he shouldn't try to make it sexy."

"But will readers be smart enough to get that?"

"The smart ones will. You have to write to the smart ones."

"Thank you," the dead writer said, and he nodded in agreement, which opened the gash where his face had been torn, and the stitches tightened.

"I can see that now. Are we leaning more toward not making it sexy?"

"I am. I think I sort of get it."

"And I'd leave the characters flat too."

"You think that's intentional?"

"Flat characters go with unsexy."

"I can see that."

"So we're changing our minds about this excerpt?"

"I am. I like it more now. I think it's going to be a big hit."

"Me too. It's brilliant."

"I wouldn't say brilliant. But it justifies itself."

"Okay, big guy. Anything you want to say?"

"Did you have my funeral yet?"

"No, you'd be in the ground."

"They're putting me in the ground?"

"You knew this. You're the one who bought the plot."

"I have to sit through my own funeral?"

"If you can hear anything in there, yes."

"It will be way better than what you just went through."

"I'd recommend not rolling around, if you can help it."

"I don't have to take these books, do I?"

"No one's going to know about the books. Closed casket."

"Because I'm deformed?"

"You're a grotesque."

"You are deformed."

"Should I look?"

"The nickel plating is reflective. Take a gander."

"I'm hideous."

"Is there anything you want to say to us before you climb back in?"

"Like what?"

"I don't know. You'll never see us again. Do you want to apologize?"

"For what?"

"For the years of insults and abuse."

"I was your teacher. I was your mentor."

"Was that the only way you knew how to do it?"

"We've all been trying to get you out of our heads. Except Maya, maybe."

"Me too. There were times when he shot me down too."

"Not in the same way."

"But in a way."

"You're all sad because I wasn't *nice* to you?"

"You could have been nice."

"You think T.S. Elliot had people being nice to him? You think Gertrude Stein was nice to Hemingway? You think Lish was nice to Ray Carver?"

"We weren't any of those people. We were still learning. We're learning still."

"It worked, didn't it? I got you to write better."

"At a certain point it was no longer about the writing. And since some of us quit, it didn't always make the writing better."

"You don't have to apologize. I think we're already getting over you. This helped a lot. You can go back in your casket. We have other stories to workshop."

"You don't want me to workshop with you? It's what I do."

"You haven't read the stories and Maya already went. You'd be unleashing your meanness for no reason."

"I won't be mean. I'll be honest."

"That's always been the excuse."

"You can take it."

"But we don't have to anymore."

"Lie down in your casket."

"Lay," he said. "I think it's lay."

"Crawl back in there."

"We don't need you anymore."

"You haven't for a long time. You're all good writers. You're my legacy."

"Lay down."

"Good night, dear prince."

"Go gentle into that good night."

"You're quoting it wrong."

"Go to sleep now."

"I want to workshop. I want to stay. I want to live."

"All of that is over, but you broke through. People will remember your books for a long time. You can sleep now."

"I wasn't sleeping in there. It's dark. It's cramped."

"Go back."

"We don't want to have to shove you inside. Please don't make us do it."

"What will you say about me?"

"He was a great writer and a good teacher."

"He loved with all his might."

"In a culture that only valued art that sold well, he was a champion of literature, and he nurtured that in us too."

"He was a sucker for a dog."

"He liked a good movie."

"We've each of us, become the writers we needed to be. He is no longer with us and he will be missed."

"So that's it?"

"You need to go."

"I don't like it in there. It's just me."

"You need to."

"Maya?"

"You can't stay. It's time to say goodbye."

§

When the last story had been talked out, and the dead writer had remained sealed up and still, they lifted the casket and put him back on the pedestal. They returned the folding chairs to their rows, they each touched the nickel lid one last time, and, with none of them crying, filed out to go rest and recharge before the memorial service. There would be more drinking tonight, though not at his house. The plan was to meet at The Hub City Grill and see if anything developed from there. They'd been workshopping for hours and were pretty much beat. They'd already said goodbye to their mentor and they were going to have to muster the energy to do so again, publicly, and with no complaints. The memorial was organized a lot like a reading, only it had a purpose.

At the public viewing, people they'd known from Petal came to pay their respects. The famous writer's girlfriend held court as people came and went. She managed the grace of a hostess, though the situation was odd, because many who arrived were people who had known the famous writer from his haunts around town, and the girlfriend wasn't used to seeing them without him being there. The owner of the Chinese restaurant, the octogenarian postal clerk he flirted with, the manager at the garden center, the kid who ran concessions at the theater. These were the people he interacted with in his life that had nothing to do with writing. None of them sought his praise or had ever asked him to write a letter of recommendation. They knew he was a writer but that was an amorphous concept, like 'Martian,' which came in many forms. They all said they were sorry to see him go and that he'd surely wait for her at the gates of heaven. None of them knew what a Minimalist was. None of them knew he was an atheist.

One of the ex-wives made an appearance and then later the second ex-wife showed up too. The first ex-wife drove down from Jackson, not too far to travel but her coming was a kindness. She'd brought her new husband, in tow, and he was a cheerful grandpa who would soon run out of steam and his impatience with his wife's loitering became apparent as she chatted on with too many of the mourners. She had worn a cape, which defined her as elegant and out of touch. The famous writer's girlfriend couldn't see the famous writer paired with her, though if she imagined back far enough she caught a glimpse of the exuberant Southern belle he'd been infatuated with, and who he'd married on a whim.

His second-wife was a literature scholar who'd flown in, unaccompanied, from Santa Fe. She was a New Yorker with no discernible accent and she and the famous writer's girlfriend got on quite well. They'd met once before, at a conference, when the girlfriend had recently achieved girlfriend status and it had been awkward, his ex feeling the slight of a man who could always start over with a younger woman. The second ex-wife seemed at least twenty years younger than the first ex-wife, who put on a show of acting young, whereas the second ex came across as more comfortable with who she was and who she'd been, even though she walked with a cane. One got the impression the second ex was steady and would remain with the living for a good long time.

"We were a good match," the second ex said to the girlfriend, "but I can see that you were a better match," which was the nicest thing anyone had said to the girlfriend in quite a while, and it was true. She would never get over the dead writer. She could hardly even remember the point when she transitioned from being his graduate student to become his equal in the relationship, and now a huge part of her was gone. She felt her legs knocked out from under her with the overwhelming realization of the famous writer's death. Over there in the nickel container was his body and the second ex-wife, who stood with a cane, was there to catch the girlfriend when she nearly fell over, and she held her up.

The famous writer's girlfriend found a seat and everyone surrounded her, until the second ex told them to back up and give her air. They sat together for a while without talking, and Trent Sanivaugh came over to join them.

"You helped write his book," he said.

"How did you know?"

"You should take credit. You should claim authorship."

"I don't know. I really *haven't* read it. He took an old manuscript of mine and dressed it up. I gave him some bricks but he built the house."

"So you have no idea how much of it is yours, or how it turned out?"

"He would talk about it sometimes. That thing was no longer mine."

"But it is."

"He has an unpublished book?" the second ex said.

"She's the co-author," Trent said.

"I knew you were a writing student," the second ex said, "but I didn't know you were a writer."

"He's the only one who has read it."

"Is it good?" the second ex wanted to know.

There were all kinds of emotions swirling in response to that question and while Trent's impulse had always been to tell the truth, he didn't want to risk saying something that might cause the famous writer to stir in his coffin. Here, with his girlfriend and his ex-wives, and all these people—it would be a disaster.

"It's good."

"Really good?" the second ex wanted to know, because when it came to books this qualification was important. If a book was good, that wasn't good enough. No one expected greatness anymore, but 'really good' meant the book was at least worth one's time.

Trent paused. Here he was with the famous writer's girlfriend, who was in mourning, and who had also been a co-author of this book. And here he was with the famous writer's second-ex, who was a literature scholar and would be able to judge the novel fairly when it came out. He had to keep the lid on the truth for a while longer, and he didn't look at either of these women but watched the nickel coffin for signs of movement.

"It's really, really good."

"I'm so glad," the second ex said.

"Me too," the famous writer's girlfriend said, and they held hands, which was uplifting to see and Trent was sure he had given them that, that if he had told them the truth about the book the air would have gone out of the room and they'd have been irritated with everything going on around them.

Trent had come back to try to convince the famous writer's girlfriend to add her name to the title page of the book, but she wasn't interested and he understood why. It was easier not to. No one was going to question his authorship of the book, but they would surely question hers, and that was something she didn't want to have to deal with.

"Have you thought about an agent?" Trent asked. "Maybe it would be better not to go with Goldman. He seemed like kind of a prick. Did you think so?"

"Whoever you think is best."

"Did you meet Holly Rorsch? She's not Goldman but she could get a good deal."

"I want you to handle that."

"I've never dealt with them before. Believe it or not after all these years I've never had someone who wanted to represent me."

"It's not hard to believe at all," the girlfriend said. "Not about you specifically, but the game."

"The fame game," the second ex added, but it wasn't funny or all too astute.

"I'm going to go now. I'll see you at the ceremony."

"Thanks for stopping by."

"I'm sorry for your loss."

§

Sparrow Walsh stood at a lectern at the side of the small chapel, with the casket draped in scarlet satin and covered with white roses. Most of the townies hadn't come back but the alumni and current writing students filled the pews. The undertaker had offered to officiate or to say a prayer, but there were so many people scheduled to stand up and read, she had politely told him 'no.'

Sparrow started with a favorite passage, one she'd told him about as she interviewed for the job at Deep South, and while flattery never worked on him, it was an unusual enough passage that he was caught off guard and remembering the passage as she recited it to him tilted his decision whether or not to hire her in her favor. As she read the passage now she spoke in a way that was self-conscious of the performance she was trying to achieve and she shouted her way through the lines, the character of the father sounding like a drill sergeant and the woman he wanted to woo, much too reluctant. It really was a beautiful passage, and a turning point for the characters in the novel, though her performance ruined it and one who wasn't already in love with that book would likely be turned off by Sparrow's reading and would never want to pick it up. When she finished they clapped politely and Sparrow went to sit down, flushed from having to stand up in front of everyone but feeling good about the passage she'd chosen.

iMOL read some doggerel he claimed would have made the dead writer laugh, and if one listened one could almost hear a muffled low guffaw coming from somewhere, until finally iMOL accidentally dropped the book he'd been reading from, and his uncomfortable reaction did get everyone laughing and the tension was lifted, so that when he found his place in the book and commenced reading doggerel again, everyone felt free to laugh in all the right places, and if there was also muffled laughter, no one heard it.

Trisha A. claimed the famous writer had been an unabashed feminist and she read a short essay that pointed out the many ways his work had achieved this. The women in his books were given equal time, equal attention, and just as much gravity and weight. He never judged his women characters for their sexuality or lack thereof, and he used gender-neutral pronouns long before it was the norm. These were the reasons she'd selected the Deep South Writers Workshop and she was sure she'd made the right decision. She concluded by saying she looked forward to his next book, where she predicted he would break new ground and finally find himself recognized as one of the great feminist writers of our time.

Maya read a shortened version of her *Atlantic Online* essay, and Allison read one of the more recognizable passages from his bestselling book. She read it well and did the book justice. She had obviously done a lot of readings over the years and it was like she was auditioning for the two agents in the room. Goldman did come away with a higher opinion of Allison after seeing her read, and Holly Rorsch made a mental note to look Allison up as soon as she had the chance to see if she were already represented by a literary agent, because she seemed to remember that she was.

Trent prefaced his reading by explaining that he had been selected to read the dead writer's last unpublished novel and he said it was quite unlike anything he'd written so far. He set up the scene by giving some character background and he tried not to watch the satin-draped coffin, which he could see out of the corner of his eye. He read a section that was different from the one he had workshopped, and because of the nature of what he was reading, he held everyone's attention. Goldman closed his eyes and turned his head to taste the words as he listened. Holly fought off the urge to turn on an audio recording app on her phone, because she was afraid the phone might beep or make some other noise. She couldn't remember if the app did that, and she wasn't going to risk it.

As he wound down his reading Trent slowed his pace, to give the passage the feel of an epiphany, though it wasn't one, but his audience responded in the way he'd hoped they would, and when he'd read the last word, "trash," they knew right away he was done, and they burst into enthusiastic applause. Trent was grateful that they'd listened and had experienced all the dead writer had wanted them to. He would never experience this kind of rapt attention when reading his own work, and he was proud that he was chosen to debut the famous writer's last book.

They filed out to their cars and Goldman, Trent, iMOL, and Scott carried the casket and loaded it into the hearse. They went to their cars and followed as a police car led the procession through the three stop lights on the way to the cemetery, through the gate and past the statue of Nathan Bedford Forrest to the section that Allison recognized because she had lain in his hole.

The mourners went to the rows of folding chairs that faced the tent over his grave as Goldman, Trent, iMOL, and Scott lifted the coffin back out and carried it over to the hoist that would lower him.

The undertaker finally made his appearance. He was a disappointment to the writers because though he was tall, his features and his dress didn't conjure the death dealer they'd hoped for. He wore a bright blue pastel shirt with a collar but no tie, only a string of large wooden prayer beads around his neck that came together over his heart where there hung a wooden cross. He had his worn Bible and the gestures and mannerisms of a Protestant minister, which he may have been at some point in his life, before he discovered the lucrative occupation of ministering for the dead.

"Please be seated," he said, and the writers and the townspeople complied.

He said, "Bow your heads," and they tilted their heads in varying degrees but again, they all complied.

He flipped a switch so the casket was lowered into the grave with an electric motor, and he read Psalm 23, which he had memorized and he only held his well-worn Bible as a prop as he lifted his other arm high, like an antenna to God, and Trent, and Allison, and iMOL, and Trisha A, and Maya all wished the undertaker wouldn't make such a show, because he risked waking up the famous writer, whom they'd all hoped was finally at rest, or that he soon would be, because burying him when he might still stir, or when he had an awareness of where he lay, seemed cruel in the extreme. None of them would speak out about it. None of them would dare articulate how they'd witnessed his defense of his excerpt and how they had to talk him into lying back down. There was no place for him anymore; he'd been wrecked, and the living would not tolerate the abomination of the dead writer who wouldn't embrace his death, and still the undertaker yammered on with the practiced inflection of a travelling revivalist, which if he didn't wind down, would raise the dead writer for sure. Allison held Scott's hand and squeezed.

Trent stared down at an ant that traversed the freshly cut grasses. iMOL tapped his foot in a way that gave away his impatience. Maya stared at the man who looked up at the heavens with an intent that he should have sensed was her wrath and her wish that he would die. Trisha A. muttered under her breath repeatedly, "Shit! Fuck! Shit!" and her hands that had until then rested on her thighs became fists that clenched and unclenched. There were as many ways to memorialize the dead as there were ways to die, but for the moment they were all stuck in a cliché. For her part, the girlfriend, who had told the undertaker to do whatever he wanted as long as it was brief, was also feeling how inappropriate it was to send the atheist off in this way, and she nearly said something, but she didn't have to because Lydia, who was a devout Christian and his secretary for the past fifteen years, and who knew him as well as anyone, got up and did what only she could. She rested a hand on the undertaker's shoulder to pull him out of his reverie, and she said, "Thank you, reverend, that will be all."

In all his years no one had ever done that to him, but Lydia projected the persona of someone people listened to, and the undertaker stopped talking and he went and sat down. Lydia flipped off the switch on the hoist, since the casket was lowered, and she invited everyone to come up and say one last goodbye to the famous writer and to throw a handful of dirt on him, which none of his current or former students was going to pass up. There was a pile of dirt by the side of the tent from where the hole had been dug, and each took a handful and tossed it down on him.

Allison invited them all to the Hub City Grill for drinks that she expected to carry them well into the night, and they drove away in their separate directions, some to their hotels or dorm rooms first, and some straight to the bar.

Once the mourners were gone, the cemetery crew dismantled the tent, folded up the chairs and they carried them over to a flatbed truck parked as near his grave as they could get. They carried away the podium and pulled up the straps from the hoist, which was also taken apart and put on the bed of the truck. The Astroturf that had been placed around the hole was picked up, shaken out, and folded up. And once the area had been completely cleared, the backhoe was brought in to fill in his grave, so there was no chance that he'd ever come crawling out. He had his place now, under a fresh mound, and in a month his stone would arrive, with the quote his girlfriend had chosen, "Less is More."

§

At the airport, when they saw each other, the writers sat together but they had nothing much else to say. They were free of any obligation. They no longer had to judge each other's writing, and they no longer had anyone but themselves to try to please. They were in possession of the email chain, so that they could contact each other if they wanted to, though they never would, because that part of their lives, when they ached so badly to become artists, was a closed chapter. Some of them had achieved success, to a degree, and some of them didn't but continued to long for it. There were a lot of them who didn't come, who had sent apologetic emails where they gave the details of their new lives, but what they were really saying was that they had given up writing, and they were okay with that. They had to do something else to make a living, and if they somehow found the time to write, and if it they were lucky enough to get it published, they still remained mostly unread since they competed with TVs, iPads, Xboxes, restaurants, movies, and the contemporary desire to never sit still. They lived in cities where there were no writers, only best-sellers and stereotypes of writers who showed up in movies with thick-rimmed glasses, plain hair, and white jackets or vintage dresses.

In closed-door meetings between the chancellor and provost author visits were discussed, but Jamaica was a long way to fly someone with very little teaching experience. Another writer who lived in Seattle wouldn't want to leave Seattle for Petal, would he? The Canadian Inuit they courted would have a better job and a better life in Canada, wouldn't he? And when it seemed there would be no one to run the Deep South Writers Workshop they ran a job ad anyway, and they asked applicants to provide a diversity statement, to explain how they would support diversity in the classroom, with the most sought-after answer being the most obvious, a short essay saying they supported diversity because they themselves were a person of color. Applications poured in from all over the country, a very diverse applicant pool, with not one application from a writer they recognized. As time wore on, the provost and the chancellor, who had at first intended to let the search committee comprised of literature professors do the job of hiring the new director, couldn't help but be disappointed by what they saw, and they cancelled the position without telling anyone. Then they cancelled the program, and by simply dissolving the Deep South Writers Workshop they created a windfall that allowed them the additional assistant football coach the Athletic Director had been clamoring for. By the time the English professors got wind of what had happened it was too late to do anything, and Sparrow, who knew she was on the outs anyway, had only managed to get a job as an adjunct at a community college. It was in Savannah, at least, and she'd saved enough to be able to move there. If she lived frugally she might be in a position to snag a tenure-track job at the community college if one ever opened up. And she could continue to apply for full-time jobs. She had Program Director on her vita now, and who knew, maybe she'd get lucky again?

In an office building that managed health insurance for the Archdiocese of Lincoln, Nebraska, where no one knew that iMOL was iMOL but they called him Jeremy, and he wore short-sleeved white dress shirts with striped ties and olive slacks, he scanned and corrected paper documents to guarantee the integrity of the electronic files in the archive, but he also went to pick up coffee and lunch orders, and he made short videos or formatted Word files into e-books whenever someone needed something like that done. There was no advancement and he mostly stayed on for the benefits. But there were times between work flows where he could get writing done in his cubicle, or he could surf for calls for manuscripts and writing contests, or he'd check in on his favorite literary satire sites, and iMOL steadily accumulated the kinds of publications that could land him a good teaching job somewhere if he'd only wanted one. Though he hadn't written anything scholarly and some search committees would see his writing as unserious, since his publications were almost exclusively online, with a lot of the magazines disappearing after five years while the paper journals coming out of the universities twice a year were exactly as they'd been forty years ago, an unchanging landscape that made him angry. Every now and then, after he'd entered a writing contest at one of these magazines they'd send him a back-issue copy and he'd flip through the stories and feel nothing but remorse for all the time, energy, and money these people had wasted. He was sorry when he heard about the cancellation of the *Deep South Triannual*, however, because that had been a good one, and pretty much the reason he had gone to graduate school there.

After the trip, the correspondence between Allison and Trent dried up. When she sat with her laptop at her workspace, Scott sometimes came up behind her and rubbed her shoulders. She often fucked around looking at Facebook while she was pretending to write and he had caught on. If he knew she wasn't writing and they were home together, he would take the opportunity to suggest that she should have sex with him, and he most commonly did this by rubbing on her shoulders. If there was a time in their relationship when she had said, "that feels good," or she'd *ooh*-ed and *ah*-ed as he massaged with his thumbs between her shoulder blades, she couldn't remember it, and so maybe this was a technique that had worked on other girls. She was annoyed that she was going to have to be blunt with him and tell him 'no,' because this was going to annoy him, and she'd been telling him 'no' a lot. It used to be, if there were something she might gain, however small, she'd give in and let him have the half hour. Returning to her workspace after that was nearly impossible, though, and these days she felt the pressure to write something great. She abandoned the story she'd been working on, which was eviscerated in the workshop and which the famous writer's girlfriend liked less than whatever Trent Sanivaugh had sent, which she would normally take as a sign this other person had an inverted aesthetic, but she'd taken the hint on this last story, one she had hoped would be the seed for a novel, and now she was between ideas, which was the worst place to be, and she had her husband Scott always pawing at her.

If she were in one of the dead writer's stories, this would be the perfect time for an affair. If she were in one of Maya Drake's stories something magical would happen, where she could stop time, hit Scott's erection with a mallet a couple of times and wake him up to tell him they'd already done it. If she were in one of her own stories, the soul-crushing weight of it all would stay with her for two hundred pages until they found a reason to love one another again and she remembered the joy of living.

She wished there was some great part-time job she could nab but she'd been so long without working she could only get a job in retail, and the pay would hardly make it worth the time. She told Scott she was still depressed about the famous writer's death. He had never had anyone like that in his life, so how could he understand? It meant there would be no more of his books, which had been a highlight for her every few years. It meant there was one fewer literary mover and shaker who knew who she was. It meant the Deep South Writers Workshop was gone and no one would ever bring it back. Very few people would understand what her experience there had meant, Scott included, and so he was going to have to let her wallow in it for the next few months.

It took a year for Trisha A. to start her own magazine because she had convinced herself she needed to hire a lawyer, and it couldn't be any lawyer, she needed a civil rights lawyer, and they tended to be busy and not interested in taking work from a fourth-wave feminist. The problem she anticipated was that her literary magazine would only publish work by women. The lawyer said you could do that without having a stated policy to that effect. She was sort of hoping it would cause controversy, and then the submissions would flow, and she'd suddenly be networking with all the best feminists in the country. But the first issue came out and no one cared. The second issue got a little more attention but mostly no one cared. Then, between the third and fourth issues the magazine got mentioned by Gloria Steinem in a TV interview, and as much as she disagreed with the kind of elitist second-wave feminist Steinem was, Trisha's inbox was awash with submissions and she suddenly and for a long while would experience the luxury of only publishing what was good. She had a magazine with some name recognition and some cachet, and she had a lot less time to write, but she had created an exclusive space for women writers. She introduced each issue in her editorial and she could comment on whatever else had been going on in the culture. She had stopped writing fiction, though now that a lot more people knew who she was the chances of publishing stories increased exponentially. She was satisfied with writing the editorial with each new issue and she imagined putting out an issue a few years down the road that was a collection of these short biting unapologetic takes on late-stage consumer capitalism. Even with success she couldn't afford to pay writers, her staff was voluntary, and she lost money with each issue, even as they sold better. She was a cocktail waitress three nights a week, as she had been since the week she turned twenty-one, and this was also enough. With the right shifts and the right shoes, she was an up-and-comer in the New York Alt-Literary scene.

Maya lived alone. Maya could live beyond her means as an associate professor with tenure who made an extra eight thousand dollars for a month of teaching each summer and an additional thirty thousand every three years with each book advance. Maya could conduct workshops in her home with her students who brought boxed wine. Maya drove an Audi convertible and she ate at Pittsburgh restaurants four or five times per week. She was also paid very well to go to Portugal each year, but because she was in Portugal, she pretty much broke even on that.

After the death of the famous writer, she became feverish in her writing, emboldened by the idea that she would one day surpass her mentor, and she wrote what she was sure had been her bravest and her best book, and her literary agent agreed, until the day the agent said she had tried, and she had tried, but there was no one else to send it to, her best book was going to remain unpublished. So instead of going out to eat—which she had maintained even as she wrote more—this latest news was such a blow she could hardly muster the strength to write at all, and she switched to getting her restaurant meals delivered. Which contributed to the clutter as Styrofoam containers and paper boxes piled up on the kitchen counter and her department chair told her she had to come to campus and couldn't conduct her workshops at home anymore. A student had complained about uncleanliness, which her chair didn't relate to her. He only said he was sorry but it was a new policy from the dean. When Maya got an idea for a book or a story she let it die, because she had already had the best idea yet, she had brought it to fruition, and the resulting manuscript was one no one wanted to publish. One of the literature professors had told her, "Couldn't you publish it yourself?" but that would be professional suicide and she'd never get promoted to full professor after that. They might even make things so she'd eventually have to leave Pitt.

To everyone who had been at the memorial, Maya had simply gone silent afterwards, which they took as a sign that she was working. They all expected that sooner or later they'd come across news of her next book, or one of her books would get made into a movie, and like everyone knew she would, Maya would shoot straight to the top.

When Trent got five advance review copies in the mail of the dead writer's book, he opened one of them, and there was his name on the title page, "with a preface by Trent Sanivaugh." What he had written was more of an impressionistic memoir-essay than a preface, but he did spell out the tenets of Minimalism for those who were unfamiliar. It was as simple as, "If you can say it in fewer words, you should." In the dead writer's formulation it had always been, "If you can say it in fewer words, then why the hell wouldn't you?" which was more words, and Trent's thesis to his preface was that underneath the old Minimalist was a stylist dying to get out, and with his last book, the famous writer had resisted the impulse to whittle everything down to toothpicks. The beauty of Minimalism was the effect it created. It demanded the writer be a disciplined self-editor and this often had the side-effect of a lyrical rhythm to the prose, which could be used to give the right passages weight, which made one seem like an important literary genius when really Minimalism had only forced one to be brief. Trent hadn't intended to write an attack on Minimalism or to join the chorus of critics who loved to say that Minimalism's time had come and gone, but as he reread his introduction now, he saw that that was exactly how it would be received.

What he had wanted was some critical distance from his mentor, especially since Trent had gotten quite good at writing Minimalist pieces himself, though no one wanted them anymore, and the dead writer had only once commended his efforts, having told him as an aside after a workshop when everyone else had left, that he shouldn't listen to his peers, and that it was clear he knew what he was doing. The dead writer told Trent that his story was as good as anything in *Vida Urbana!* by Rabe Thelm, who had revived Minimalism for the Modern Era, the one they all looked up to, and it was the highest compliment Trent could have ever received from his mentor. Kurtz immediately followed up by saying that nothing else Trent had written was as good as that particular story, and if he had any hopes of being a writer he had to figure out a way to do that same thing again and again. But he also told Trent it was too late for Minimalism. He was good enough, but he would have to figure out something else, since there was no new Minimalist revival on the horizon.

His introductory essay that dismantled Minimalism felt like a betrayal as he read it over again. He hadn't even known he was doing that. And the essay was good enough that he could continue this approach and make it his shtick as he became a literary critic, finally landing a tenure-track job teaching Modern and contemporary American literature, fiction-writing be damned. And why the hell wouldn't he?

For all these years it was the one compliment from his mentor, when he compared him to Thelm, that had propelled him. All the rejections from magazines, literary agents, and publishers. All the lost time spent reading, and the time spent typing at a laptop. He would finally have his name on the spine of a book, and it was because someone had died. And all the while he had done it because this dead guy had once told him he was as good as Thelm. So he knew all the literary magazine editors and all the literary agents that had rejected him over the years had been wrong. Maya Drake and Allison Avett had been wrong. The dead writer had never given either of them that kind of compliment. He was good enough, and as long as Trent continued to write, eventually someone in a position who could make a difference would recognize what was special about him.

He called up his girlfriend, as he had promised, to tell her the advance copies had arrived.

"They're here," he said. "They're really real. And my name is on the title page."

"On the title page?" she said. "Didn't they put your name on the cover?"

"These are advance copies," he said. "They don't really have covers. They put plain paperback covers on them with minimal graphics. They want to keep costs down because they give them away. These are what they send to reviewers and bloggers to try to create buzz."

"You'll get your name on the cover, when it comes out?"

"I think so."

"You're not sure?"

"I think I'm sure. I think so."

"That will be something, won't it?"

About the author

John Minichillo's novel, *The First Woman on Mars* is forthcoming from Spaceboy Books. His novel, *The Snow Whale*, was an Independent Publishers Book Awards regional gold medalist for the West-Pacific and an Orion Magazine Book Prize notable. He wrote the column, "How to Be a Better Teacher-Person Through Apathy" at McSweeney's Internet Tendency as one of the winners of their column contest.

His science fiction novel, *EOB: Earth Out of Balance*, out now on Kindle Press, was described as 'one of the smartest, funniest, best-developed novels of any genre.'

John is the recipient of a Tennessee Individual Artists Grant and lives and teaches in Nashville.

About the publisher

HYBRID Ink, LLC began in 2018 with it's inaugural publication, Jen Durbent's *My Dinner With Andrea*. Borne out of a desire to see more of the publications they loved, Madison Scott-Clary and the editors at HYBRID Ink made it their goal to provide well-versed and sophisticated works of fiction, poetry, and creative non-fiction.

We want writing that gets us thinking about ourselves, stories that span genres, and words that change the way we look at the world.

www.ingramcontent.com/pod-product-compliance
Lightning Source LLC
Chambersburg PA
CBHW071155180726
48291CB00007B/2472